The Otters of Ruapuke

The Otters of Ruapuke

by

Rob Robinson

Illustrations by

Hilary Robinson

iUniverse, Inc.
New York   Bloomington

The Otters of Ruapuke

iUniverse books may be ordered through booksellers or by contacting:

iUniverse
1663 Liberty Drive
Bloomington, IN 47403
www.iuniverse.com
1-800-Authors (1-800-288-4677)

Because of the dynamic nature of the Internet, any Web addresses or links contained in this book may have changed since publication and may no longer be valid. The views expressed in this work are solely those of the author and do not necessarily reflect the views of the publisher, and the publisher hereby disclaims any responsibility for them.

ISBN: 978-1-4502-2349-2 (pbk)
ISBN: 978-1-4502-2350-8 (ebookk)

Library of Congress Control Number: 2010904810

Printed in the United States of America

iUniverse rev. date: 4/15/10

Prelude

The Anthropologist was puzzled. He called his assistant over.

"I've been trying to figure this out for days," he said. His owlish eyes squinted behind the thick lenses he wore. "And just where have you been, anyway?"

His Assistant, who was young and hardworking, rolled her eyes. "You sent me to the Maori, the local tribe in New Zealand, to try and find answers, remember?"

Searching his memory, the Anthropologist finally nodded. "Oh, yes. Well, what did you find? How do they explain a colony of sea otters here in the Southern Hemisphere when the creatures are supposed to be in the Northern?"

"Well, according to the Maori they weren't brought her by the Europeans."

That had been the Anthropologist's theory, and his eyes widened. "Oh, what other possible explanation could there be?"

She shrugged. "They say the colony was already here when the Europeans arrived."

"Impossible," he snorted. "Do they think otters would migrate here? These creatures have thick fur, they hate the heat, and yet you're suggesting they would somehow make their way

Rob Robinson

down tropical waters and blazing sun because they knew they would come to a cold climate again? Don't be absurd."

His Assistant sighed. Her boss could be so unreasonable when facts didn't match his opinions. She'd spent a lot of time gaining the trust of the Maoris just to get the story she was sharing with him. She believed it to be true.

"They say giant ships came with people they now believe were Chinese and the otters were aboard these ships. One wrecked off the coast here and the people and the otters stayed."

"Giant ships! Absurd. I've seen Chinese junks. I wouldn't for a minute call them giant. Or even big."

"They say the wreck was longer than their village," she continued, sticking to her story. "Like a football field." She meant, of course, what Americans call a soccer field.

The Anthropologist shook his head. "They exaggerate, you know. Build everything up over time to match what they wanted to happen. Besides, what would a Chinese junk be doing with live otters? They might carry otter furs, but not a cargo of the little beast. Impossible to manage, you know. Makes no sense. No, it must have been the Europeans. We'll find the answer for ourselves."

Of course, the Anthropologist was wrong. There had been giant ships, as large as modern ocean liners, a fleet of them in fact. A fleet that had traveled the world long before Columbus or Magellan had even dreamed of doing so. And they did carry live otters...and so much more.

Chapter 1   How the trouble began

The old Emperor died.

First only those in the palace knew, but soon the whole kingdom. And the men who had hated him rejoiced.

"Did you hear?" They asked each other in private. "Now we can get what we want."

"No, wait," some among them cautioned, "we will have the young son do it for us, as soon as he becomes Emperor."

And so the young Emperor's advisors waited while the ceremonies of pomp and splendor took place. There were parades and fireworks, grand feasts and festivals. Then the kingdom settled down once again, and the advisors went to see the young Emperor, whom they had carefully groomed when he was only a prince, to reap the harvest of their labors.

They came to the palace in the abominable Forbidden City that the old Emperor had built, hating it but willing to endure. It could remain, for the young Emperor liked it, but all else must go.

They waited while he came into the great hall and sat upon his throne, their heads bowed to the ground, on their knees before the greatest Emperor in all the world, the Emperor of China. The young man wore the royal silken robes of office, brilliant and beautiful. He sat on the magnificent throne, and he waited.

"Your eminence," the one they had chosen as spokesman began, "you bring joy to all of us to finally see your royal presence upon the throne."

He nodded, encouraging them to speak on, knowing there would be much more.

"But soon the royal fleet your father had built will be returning."

He nodded again, but this time he wore a scowl upon his face. His father's fleet, the old Emperor who he had detested, would return and bring glory to his father. There would be treasures from afar and glories in the stories, and the people would be reminded of his father and not think of him. He winced thinking of it.

"What should I do?" He asked.

They had been waiting for that question. "The ships will be loaded with treasure. Bring it to the palace here and keep it for yourself. There will also be records, ship's logs and maps and charts. If you allow them to be seen, all of China will exclaim over your father's deeds, your father's fleet, your father's discoveries. No one will remember you. Everyone will only want to read about the foreign lands your father found."

The young Emperor's eyes narrowed, his brow furrowed. He had hated his father, who had never treated him with love or respect. The thought of everyone talking about the old man while he sat here on the throne, ignored and unnoticed nearly drove him blind with rage.

"I will have them destroyed!" He cried out. He did not notice the smiles carefully hidden by the men before him. "When they return, all the charts, all the maps, all the ship's logs, every record of them will be burned. And the ships," he added, as the thought occurred to him. "No more such ships will be made. No more will be needed. China does not need foreigners or their goods. We are the Middle Kingdom, and our tribute nations around us are enough."

It was what they had wanted. But the young Emperor was not done.

"The crews," he added, "must be sent to work on farms, never to remember the sea again. And the animals," he remembered the stories that his father's advisors had told, extolling the great deeds of even the animals in his father's kingdom, "there are dogs and otters and such on board the ships, are there not?"

The men were puzzled. They had not thought of these. "Yes, Emperor, there are."

"The dogs will be slaughtered, and the otters, too, and their furs taken. From now on, otters will only be used for their furs. I have spoken. See that it is done immediately upon their return."

He rose and left, wishing to be finished thinking of this for now. He did not even wait to hear their hurried, "It will be done as you say."

Nor did he see the smiles on all their faces. It was even more than they had expected, more than they had come for.

When all had left, the eunuchs and the advisors waiting only for the door to signal the Emperor's departure from the room to also leave, the great hall stood empty, the last echo of fading footsteps the only sound. The footsteps echo bounced for a little time around the rich, brown beams of wood that held up the magnificent ceiling. Then it, too, faded away. Though, the room wasn't quite empty.

There next to the Emperor's throne stood a carefully crafted bamboo cage. Within it perched a small mockingbird. Her name was Huan, which means happy and joyous. The name suited her, for that was her job, to bring joy and happiness to the Emperor when he requested song. She did her job well, for she sang beautifully, and she made the Emperor happy.

Like all mockingbirds, Huan had no songs of her own. All her songs she would steal from the other birds in the royal garden. She knew that those birds resented her for this, so she tried as hard as she could to be their friend. When the Chief Eunuch placed her cage in the window that overlooked the royal garden each afternoon, she would repeat the gossip of the court, and the birds would gather to hear her words. She enjoyed their rapt attention, much more in fact than the attention of the Emperor, even. For the birds were here peers, and one always likes to be admired by one's peers.

She waited in her perch now, marveling at the words she had just heard. What lovely gossip to share. This must be savored, then parceled out slowly, she decided. Won't they find me wonderful now?

Chapter 2   A carefree life no more

Yong felt the waves roll over and around him. They were strong waves, good waves. Far to his right he saw the net, the cork bobbing where it held one end up in the water. To his left floated his friend Xun, waiting with him for the school to near the surface.

They were both sea otters, wonderful creatures of land and sea who naturally preferred the sea. Nearly four feet in length and weighing almost as much as a healthy sled dog, their sleek and glistening fur attested to a good diet and plenty of exercise, surprising since they had been traveling on board ship now for more than two years. But the ships were unique, the largest in the world, the largest the world would see for centuries to come. The otters, eight of them onboard this ship alone, lived together in the hold but swam in the sea regularly, hunting for schools of fish to herd to the nets of their masters on board the ship, hunting food for the crew, themselves and all the other creatures on board.

"Here they come," Xun exclaimed, diving exuberantly in the water and surfacing to splash Yong.

Yong laughed, looked down and saw, sure enough, the school of fish they had seen headed this way were now close enough to herd. He and Xun swam very quickly on top of the waves until they had reached the back of the school, then they dove. Down, down they dove until they were as deep as the school, brightly flashing scaled heads and tails in a group too numerous to count, each at least half as long as the two otters.

Holding their breaths, they flashed each other hand signals and began to work. Each of them took on the task of herding, nipping tails with their razor sharp teeth, tickling fins with their paws until the crazed fish swam into the backs of those ahead of them, sending their fellows into a frenzy of motion. Soon the whole school raced forward, trying to elude these mad hunters at their tails.

Expertly Yong and Xun worked them towards the net, invisible to the fish until the last moment when it was too late. The waiting human crew began pulling on the corners of the net, bringing up hundreds of wildly flapping and diving fish, caught now.

The two otters surfaced then, blowing out and gasping in great chunks of fresh air. They capered around, diving and laughing, cheering at their success.

"We are great hunters!" The two crowed.

On the other side of the ship three of their comrades, working another net and waiting for a school to approach, heard them. Bao, a young female who often played with Yong and Xun, smiled. Her two female companions groaned, though.

"We must hurry and equal them or there will be no living with them tonight at dinner," Huang, who was older and no longer hung around the younger ones since she had given birth to a pup last season, sighed.

Mei, the other female, nodded. "Especially Yong," she said, "I can hear him now bragging about what a fisherman he is. Still," she admitted, "he is cute."

Bao agreed, but didn't say so. Yong was her particular friend. He had helped her when she'd first arrived, having been stolen from her family and put onboard ship as the fleet was leaving. She hadn't known any of the others and had been in despair and lonely. But Yong had quietly helped her learn the craft of driving schools of fish to the nets, listened to her talk of her parents and siblings lost off the coast of China, and been a true friend.

But, she smiled to herself, that wasn't to say that he didn't love to brag about his fishing ability. She knew Huang was right, they must make a good catch or there would be no living around him until the next chance to fish.

They'd been waiting for a long time, though, and hadn't spotted a school as Yong and Xun had. She decided to take action. "Huang, you stay here while Mei and I find a school and bring it to you." She didn't wait for an answer but flipped around in the water and began swimming out to sea. In moments Mei was swimming beside her.

The two moved quickly and easily through the water, traveling right through large waves and never wasting any motion. Otters are a wonder in the water, able to glide, swim and dive as if they were fish and not mammals. Soon they were far from the giant ship that had been their home these two years.

As they swam Bao kept scanning under and on top of the water, looking for signs of a school of fish. Then she saw it. A large perch leapt out of the waves and skimmed over the water, then another and another. Mei saw it. "Yes, let's bring them to the ship."

They dove at the same time, located the large school and using gestures, told each other what they would do. Splitting off, they soon were each on an outside of the school and began to nip and slap at the rear members of the school. Soon the whole frightened mass of fish were frantically swimming to get away from them, right for the nets and the waiting Huang.

In no time an exhausted but happy Bao watched as the humans hauled a bulging net aboard the ship. "There," she smiled, "that should show Yong."

"It certainly should," a familiar voice sang out. She jumped. There he swam behind her, grinning from ear to ear.

She splashed him. "You startled me!"

yong

He laughed. "Easy to do when you're busy admiring how wonderful you are. Quite a school," he pointed at the nets.

"It is," she admitted, proudly.

"At least half of what we brought in, wouldn't you say Xun?" He asked his partner.

"Maybe half," Xun said grudgingly, "more likely a third."

Bao felt her fur stand up. "Why you conceited pups! You know it's as good as yours. Look at how the net is nearly breaking with the weight of the fish."

"Scrawny net," Xun told her.

"Yes," Yong agreed, "probably ready to break."

She dove for him then, dunking his head under the salty water and holding him until he moved impossibly quickly and she found herself under him, being dunked. They wrestled in the water for a few minutes, then both let go and came up for air, laughing.

Huang chirped disapproval at them. "Would you two stop it? You're like two pups in a litter."

"He started it," Bao began, then was interrupted by Mei.

"Look at that bird!" She exclaimed.

Coming to them, seemingly walking on the water, wings outspread, was a delicate, dark-winged bird with a band of white at its tail. They all paddled and watched, amazed as it did a dance on the surface of the waves, looking for all the world like it was, indeed, walking on the water.

When it came within a few feet of them it balanced on its webbed feet, wings spread and stared at them. "Hello, hello, hello," it chirped. "Are you otters, otters?"

They all fought not to burst out laughing. Yong answered first. "Yes, we are, friend bird. And what might you be?"

"I'm a petrel, a petrel," it answered, "name's Stormy, Stormy. Heard about you. Thought I should come, come."

"Heard about us?" Huang asked, "From who?"

The little bird cocked its head, ducked it under a wing for a moment. "From albatross. He heard from gull, he said. Sparrows told gulls. They heard from Emperor's mockingbird herself. Herself."

Suddenly the bird had all their attention. Though they were otters and took little notice of pomp and such nonsense that humans enjoyed, they knew about the Emperor. He had sent them on this voyage, after all.

"Is he well, our old Emperor?" Huang asked.

Stormy circled them, his feet skimming the waves. "Not old, not old. Young, young. New Emperor. Old Emperor died. Died."

Xun snorted. "That young pup? He never liked our fleet I heard. I wonder what he will do with us?"

Stormy answered, "Fleet is to be undone, undone."

Bao smiled. "Maybe we'll be let go then, and I can go home."

"Like to see the coast again," Yong nodded. "Maybe my parents are still there."

But Stormy began beating his wings in agitation. "No, no. Not home, not home. All dogs will be killed, all otters skinned for fur, for fur."

Everyone fell silent, stunned. They could hear the humans on board ship shouting orders, slapping the fish against the deck before gutting them. Then the first guts began to fly overboard and into the water. Stormy left them then to get some dinner. The otters didn't move.

"Could it be true?" Mei whispered. "Would the humans do such a barbaric thing?"

Just then they heard a voice shouting at them, and a sound of hands drumming upon the wooden hull of the ship. They saw Shen-si, the human who had trained them and who was in charge of them, beating his hands frantically on the side of the ship shouting as loudly as he could.

It was Huang who brought them to their senses. "Quick," she ordered, "we must not dawdle here. The blood and guts will attract the sharks."

Then the sight of the fish guts floating in the water where Stormy busily gorged himself awakened the memory in them. Otters fear sharks, as well they might, for the deadly killers like nothing better than to snatch an unwary sea otter from the water for a snack. They knew the blood would be like a siren, calling the sharks to come and feast. The human crew already had poles out, for they loved shark meat and would catch as many as they could.

They all began to swim quickly for the basket that Shen-si had lowered by rope for them. He danced now above it, holding onto the rope with two strong crewmen at his side, ready to haul them aboard. They were near it when Yong felt more than saw the gigantic, white presence powering through the water underneath them.

"Swim as hard as you can," he ordered, then deliberately splashed and dove away from them.

"Yong!" Bao cried, but Huang snapped her teeth at her.

"He is giving us a chance. Swim for the basket, it's a giant white one."

The giant white sharks were the most feared of sea creatures. Otters are lightning fast in the water, but the whites are just as fast. This one would have gulped them up in the next moment if Yong had not distracted it. Now it lunged at the brave otter who swam in a zig-zag pattern away from the others. Yong felt the rush of water displaced by the giant body chasing him, then a cruel snap of jaws just missing his rear legs as he dove sharply to the right. The shark had guessed wrong, but it turned so quickly he had no time to feel even a moment of relief as it came at him again.

The others, meanwhile, had reached the basket and clambered on board. Shen-si began to haul them up. "No," Bao barked, and the others took up the same cry. The humans had never bothered to learn their tongue, as the otters had learned to understand the humans, but Shen-si knew their frantic barkings meant something was amiss. Peering over the side, he saw the churning, white water of the great shark's powerful lunges at Yong, and then saw the little otter dodging the giant.

"Hold up," he ordered the two crewmen helping him with the rope, "wait for my order."

He saw the little otter leap out of the water, the snapping jaws following him in a frenzy of hate and rage, saw the razor-sharp teeth miss and clash together with a sound that echoed across the water, then Yong was swimming as furiously as he could for the basket and his waiting friends. It hung several feet in the air where Shen-si had halted it, and they all wondered if Yong could even leap that high.

So did he. But he gathered all of his muscles and powered himself towards it, leaping at the last instant for safety. His leap was not quite enough, though, and he reached helplessly inches short of the top rim. Just as he began to fall back, his friends reached over the side and pulled him aboard.

Shen-si yelled, "Pull, pull," and the two crewmen jerked the basket upwards. Just then the great monster shark burst out of the water reaching its body high, its gaping jaws revealing row upon row of gleaming, eager teeth. For a moment they all feared it would swallow the entire basket, but the crewmen gave one mighty pull and the basket leapt up, the jaws came together, "Snap!" just below it, the basket was hauled aboard, the monster fell back to the sea, thrashing the water in a white foaming spasm of disappointment.

Yong collapsed into the arms of his friends. "Thank you," he breathed.

Xun laughed. "And thank you, my crazy friend. We thought you were a meal for sure."

"Don't ever do that again," Bao cried, hugging him close. "Whatever came over you to do that?"

He shivered. "I don't know. It just seemed the thing to do at the time."

"You saved our lives," Mei said quietly, "he would have gobbled us up one by one if you hadn't lured him away."

"Yes," Huang agreed, "but if that little bird was right, who will save us from the new Emperor?"

They stared at her. They had quite forgotten Stormy and his warnings. No one spoke, and a shiver went down each spine. The fate that awaited when the great ships returned was again on their minds. So it was a sober group of otters who were led to their home below ship.

Chapter 3 How friend Ling
became an ally

The rat cringed. It held tightly to the armful of rice it had managed to grab. Its name was Ling, and while he wasn't the most cunning of the rats aboard ship, he was the quickest and the best at finding food. He had located a bowl someone of the crew had left out, with a small bit of rice uneaten from dinner. Ling had clutched it tightly and made his way in the shadows towards the open knot in the deck's wood that led to a beam he could take down to his friends. That's when he'd heard the sound.

Pug. It had to be Pug. He was the only one of the dogs small enough and clever enough to have gotten this close to Ling without being heard. The scratch of one nail on the wood, a sound no one but Ling would have noticed, had warned him. When the rat froze, Pug must have halted also. Which meant he had smelled Ling, but not sighted him. There was still a chance.

Ling stuffed the rice in the small bag he carried like a knapsack on his back. From it he took a worn, white bone. It had long lost all flavor, at least to a rat, but Ling knew for a dog it was different. He'd held onto it for some time, just in case of an emergency.

"Can't get more emergency than this," Ling muttered to himself. Shifting the bone from hand to hand, he waited to hear something he could aim at. If he had patience, he knew he would.

"Snuff," came the sound. Ling almost chuckled, but fear held that in. Dogs can't help it, he thought, they have to smell things and do it just that way. It was to his right, a little over...he tossed the bone in that direction. It landed with a satisfying clicking sound and rolled across the deck.

"Err...ruff!" Came the expected growl, the sound of a pounce, the crunch as teeth closed on the bone. Ling didn't wait for more. Scurrying as fast as his paws would carry him, he ran for the knothole. He heard an angry yelp as Pug spotted him, then the frantic clicking of nailed paws on the wooden boards of the deck as Pug scrambled to catch him. The little dog was lightning quick, but Ling had a head start. Just before Pug's jaws closed around his tail, he disappeared down the hole.

Pug's face appeared at the hole peering down as Ling glanced back. "It's you, Ling, isn't it?" Pug sniffed.

"Yes, noble rat catcher," Ling softly answered.

"I missed this time, but I'll get you yet," Pug promised.

"I'm afraid you might," Ling whispered, more to himself than to the dog, and scurried away.

A large dog with a lion's mane of fur and a black tongue appeared than, dwarfing the little Pug. "You were too slow," Bok growled.

"No, he was too clever," Pug answered, pride making him resent the larger dog's accusation, "I got the bone he threw, and it gave him a moment to run. Even then, I almost had him. It was Ling. That's means

they are becoming desperate, for he is their best, and all he found was a little rice."

"Chow will be angry you missed him," Bok snarled.

Pug growled in his throat. Bok was a killer, and he had only one thought at a time. Pug thought of himself as a hunter, a trained professional for whom catching rats was a fine vocation. He did not always kill, though he often did. Sometimes, if they were close to a shore, he would toss the caught rat overboard and let it try to swim for its life. He had a sense of fairness that way. Bok did not. Bok lived only for the kill, and had no sympathy for anything else.

"Let Chow catch him, then," Pug muttered, but not too loudly. He feared Chow, whose cold intelligence made him much deadlier than Bok's killer instincts. Before Bok could think to ask Pug to speak up, Pug had gone, his paws rapidly click-clicking away.

Bok sniffed for any more rats, found none, than turned with narrowed eyes and made his own way to the front of the ship where he and Chow lived. He found his chief staring out at the bow, sniffing the breeze that flowed from the sea.

"One of the great white killers almost ate our otters," Chow spoke in his low, deep voice. Bok listened. "They were careless after the hunt. Something about a bird. It would be well to find out what had their attention."

Bok sniffed. "Otters," he said the word with disdain, "their attention is taken by anything and everything. Frivolous, careless creatures..." he stopped and gnawed at one paw, than licked it.

"They won't tell us," Chow continued as if Bok had not spoken, as indeed his words had meant nothing, only feelings brought to the surface, "but they like Shih. I will ask the little one to talk to them, to find out."

"Shih," Bok had disdain again in his tone, "that one talks and the wind makes more sense." He went to the pile of rope, carefully coiled, and nosed in it until he found the bone he'd placed there the other day. He began to gnaw at it, working it over lovingly, growling with pleasure as his teeth sharpened on it's hard surface.

Chow glanced at Bok to make sure of the bone he had. Chow, too, had hidden one in the ropes. He sniffed. It was not his. "Nevertheless, they talk to him. I will go ask him." He left Bok crunching happily.

"Yong," the otter heard his name called as he ducked into the low area where his kind were kept. They had made it into a den, seaweed, dried now, for nesting places, a cleaned area where the fish could be eaten without soiling the sleeping spots. He sniffed, knew it had been Hui who had called. He waited for his eyes to adjust to the gloom.

Xun had been right behind him. "They will be worried," he whispered, "the others must have spoken."

Yong knew he was right. The three females would have rushed in with all the news. He could imagine how Hui and Zan, Huang's mate, would have reacted. When his eyes allowed him to pick them out he made his way to them.

"They told you of the messenger bird?" He asked.

Zan grabbed at the fur on Yong's front paw. "They told us of the white killer who almost had you for dinner. You were foolish, and brave." He sighed. "And you saved them all. Thank you, Yong."

"But what of the bird?" Hui, the wise old female otter whom they all looked to for the correct way, and to keep their paths steady, asked. "It told of trouble." This last not a question.

"What did they tell you?" Yong asked, for he did not wish to repeat what had already been said.

Hui related the story of the new Emperor and his order that all of them must die. Her tone begged him to say it was not so. Yong only wished that he could.

"Yes, those were his words."

Hui sighed. "And you believe this petrel, this bird of the long flying?"

Petrels were known to the otters, for they often returned from long flights at sea with wondrous stories. As a pup, Yong remembered listening in awe, wondering at ever seeing such things. Now he had been at sea for two years, had seen all of it, and he no longer wondered. He merely wished to go home.

"I believe. When I was young I would listen to their stories and only half believe, for they spoke of things impossible to conceive. But," he waved a paw to include them all, "we have seen such things, and every story that we heard, every story I ever heard," he amended, "was proven true on this voyage we have taken."

And they all nodded in agreement.

"What shall we do, Yong?" It was Bao, her voice quivering.

"I do not know," he answered truthfully.

"To not know is to be one with all living things," a voice came behind them. They whirled to see Shih the small priest dog entering the den. "Only enlightenment can bring wisdom."

Shih was half the size of the female otters, with white curly hair streaked with black and gray. His small face seemed pushed in, and his little pink tongue forever flicked out as if to taste the air. Of all the dogs, they feared him least, respected him most, were almost friends. But still, he remained a dog.

"What brings you down among the lowly otters, Shih?" Asked Hui.

Shih bowed to her as an elder, then smiled. "News of your remarkable escape from the white killer reached me. I came to see if all was well."

"It is."

"And, there was also a story of a bird who brought important news."

Yong's ears pricked up. How much did the dogs know? He wondered. Shih stood, waiting for them to speak, and Yong guessed that he knew no more than what he had just shared.

"Petrels fly far. We asked for news of home. All is well," Yong replied.

Shih frowned. "Is that all? You're sure there was not more. You seem..." he paused, seeming to weigh the air around them, "unduly upset," he finished.

Xun laughed, a short bark that echoed around them. "You escape a white killer's lunging jaws snapping the air right beneath you and see if you are not upset."

"You are sure that is all?"

"That is all, friend Shih," Hui spoke for all of them, wishing the small canine to be gone, "you may tell that to your master, Chow."

Shih did not take offense, but the jibe hit home. "I will leave you, then. Until we speak again." And he departed.

Mei spoke up for the first time since Yong had come in. "The dogs, too, are to die. Perhaps we should share the news with them."

"They won't believe you," a voice said. All of them recognized it.

"Friend Ling," Yong laughed. "How long have you been listening?"

"To all of it," Ling showed himself from the edge of the meal area where fish heads remained as the last of their meal, waiting for new fish from the recent catch to be dumped down the hole above it, a long shaft from the cargo hold above, by the humans.

Bao giggled. "That explains why no one smelled you. Those fish heads have become ripe."

Ling smiled. "It seemed a safe place to be."

"You may take the heads," Hui told him. The otters had been feeding the rats in this way for some time. They knew of the dogs' vigilance, of Pug's huntings, and they sympathized. That Ling had waited for permission raised his esteem in their eyes. They watched him now, but he did not immediately pick up a head and go.

"What will you do now?" He asked.

Hui shrugged. "We do not know. We will talk much, but some things we cannot control."

"You could escape when they let you free to hunt," Ling suggested.

Huang spoke up. She had run to her pup when she first came in, and had been playing with its gambling form ever since. Pipi no longer nursed, and Zan played with him when she was away. But as all otters do, she loved her pup deeply and enjoyed frisking with him. Now she had paused to tell Ling what truly kept them all on board ship. "Only if we were close to shore. Otherwise we would be a meal before we reached land. Besides," she glanced at her mate, Zan, "we cannot leave behind those down here. And the humans always make sure there are some down here to make us stay."

The brown rat picked up a fish head, sniffed it, put it down and tried another. He seemed to be thinking. "You have a problem. If you stay they will take you home and you will die. And you won't leave without all going. You are good people, otters."

"Thank you, friend rat," Hui said, encouraging him, for she could feel that he had more to say.

"While the ship is intact, then, you are trapped." The rat seemed almost to be thinking aloud. "Then, of course, that must be changed. The ship, I believe, must crash against the rocks of land, and then you can all escape as it breaks apart. Dangerous, but we rats have done it before on other ships, in other times."

He was silent, watching them. Bao looked to Yong, who felt her gaze, returned it and shrugged. The otters all waited for Hui, whose wisdom they respected. She had a puzzled expression, and finally her head came up from staring at the deck. "Some of the ships of the fleet have wrecked against the rocks of shores, but they were piloted by humans who were careless. Our humans are not so. I do not believe they will wreck this ship."

Her gaze now carried a question to Ling. "What is your answer to that?" it said.

"True," he nodded. He nibbled at the fish head he held, smiled that it was acceptable, and prepared to leave. He shoved it up ahead of him in the knothole that led up a tunnel he would use. Before he disappeared after it, he spoke. "It would seem, then, that you must gain control of the ship and crash it yourselves." And he was gone.

Chapter 4

Meeka, too, lived down in the cargo hold. Her home was much bigger than the otters' den. She had plenty of leaves and branches to munch on, but she did grow lonely from time to time. The otters would visit, but they scarcely could sit still and so did not stay for long. The only one who really came to stay and talk was Sharpe.

The faint creaking of boards told her that someone approached. By the weight, by the timing of the measured tread, the sound of the slight pad-pad and occasional click of nails, she knew it to be Sharpe. Still munching on leaves, for she must eat all the time to maintain herself on a diet only of vegetation, she waited for her friend. Streaks of light from overhead, like small rays of sun that danced in with dust swimming in their beams, gave her enough illumination to see when he appeared at the entrance to her space.

Sharpe, his soft, brown fur glistening each time a ray of light passed across it, came in, sat at her feet, and waited for her to finish chewing, his happy tongue lolling out and his crinkled eyes smiling.

"Hello, Sharpe," she finally said.

He snorted and clutched his nose between his two forelegs, rubbing it a moment. Then he looked up. "I came to see how you were."

"Lonely," she answered truthfully.

"I thought as much." He glanced around the enclosure, noted the wetness of the walls from the bilge just below their deck as the vessel leaked more and more the longer the voyage grew and the more the waves and storms pounded it gradually apart. "Do they ever bring you up on deck for some sun?"

Meeka shook her head. "Not for some time. When I was a new curiosity, some time ago after I was captured, they would. Other ships would come alongside and beg to see me. But now," she shrugged, "I am grateful they remember my food."

The gentle dog came over and sniffed at it. "Still just leaves?"

"It's what I like."

"I couldn't," he said, only half out loud. She didn't mind.

They both heard a noise then, and watched the small opening at the end of one wall. It led down to the otters' den, so they weren't surprised when in tumbled Yong and Bao, wrestling and laughing. That didn't surprise them either; the otters were always like that, it seemed. Meeka liked that about them. They were fun and livened her lonely days.

"Good to see you, Yong. Bao."

They untangled and began to say hello back to their friend, then noticed Sharpe.

"Sharpe," Bao exclaimed, "what are you doing here?"

"The same as you, visiting a friend."

But Yong and Bao now stood, uncertain what to do. They had come to share their news with Meeka. She was a good friend, and often had wisdom to see the sides of something they had never considered. But Sharpe, though he was the friendliest of the dogs and most liked by the otters, still was a dog. They weren't sure where the dogs would stand with what they now knew.

Meeka towered over the two otters, she towered over all the animals aboard. She was a Mylodon, a giant sloth, a creature soon to be extinct, though she did not know that and would have laughed at the thought. There were many of her kind in the bottomlands of South America where the great Chinese fleet had found her. They had captured her with Chow and Bok and with great nets, hauling her aboard as a curiosity to be taken back to their emperor. If she died they would exhibit her fur, but they preferred to show her off alive, so her food had been stored carefully and given out to her in generous portions. Sloths were not unknown to the Chinese, though one of this size had never before been seen.

"You came to tell me something?" Meeka asked intuitively.

Yong hesitated. "Yes," he softly intoned, staring at Sharpe.

Sharpe sighed. "You would like me to leave. This is not for my ears I take it."

Mention of his ears, those short, floppy brown ears that so matched his wrinkly hide, made the two otters bark with laughter. And it changed Yong's mind. His eyes met Bao's; she could see his question dance in his pupils. She nodded, yes.

"You may stay, friend Sharpe. Though, perhaps you will think first before you share this with your other canine companions?"

Sharpe's tongue lolled out again and he grinned. "They do not often share with me, so I will take my time deciding whether to share with them."

They nodded at that. He had mentioned before how different he felt from them, how differently they treated him. "It concerns something we learned today while hunting fish," Yong began. Then he proceeded to share all the story of the little petrel and the news it had brought. At the pronouncement of the old emperor's death, Sharpe's smile turned to a frown. Then when he learned of the new young emperor's decisions, a growl escaped his lips.

"He would kill us dogs, too, you say?" He asked.

"This I heard."

"Grumpf!" He snorted. He chewed at one paw thoughtfully. He looked up. "Chow will not want to believe it. And if Chow does not believe it, neither will Bok. Shih will wait to see how the others think. And Pug..." he shook his head. His wrinkled skin continued to shake a moment after he stopped. Yong and Bao watched it, fascinated.

Meeka had taken to chewing some more leaves as the story had commenced. It wasn't that she did not care, it was just that her metabolism needed to be fed. Now she paused, and totally unlike herself, spoke with food half chewed. "What of Pek?" She asked.

Pek was the captain's dog, small and spoiled. He kept to himself, feeling superior to the others. Chow and Bok hated him, and the others had given up trying to be his friend. But Sharpe he tolerated, and now the wrinkled brown dog thought about him.

"He would be a good one to have on our side. He knows where things are in the ship. If we are to control it and run it aground, he would be essential."

Bao squealed, a paw to her mouth in excitement. "You are with us on this, then Sharpe?"

His eyes opened in surprise. "It seems I am. I did not know it until just now. But I do not wish to be slaughtered, and maybe a new land will be exciting. Besides," he regarded Meeka warmly, "my friend should be free again."

Snitch's eyes narrowed. This must be reported to Bruno, he knew. He decided he had heard enough, that nothing more important would be said. Quickly he turned and scurried up the beam he had come down. He had been listening from the end of it, where a knothole opened onto Meeka's home. Bruno had ordered him to find out what had happened with the otters, all the talk since before dinner had been about their near encounter with the great white killer. Now he knew more, and he savored knowing it.

The little rat, a runt who would long ago have been dead had he not mastered the skill of being necessary to Bruno, now had something that he could use to bargain with all sides. He smiled as he hurried to where his band of rats hung out.

Chapter 5

The fish head had become quite a burden by the time Ling managed to wrestle it to Li's. Her room seemed to have just lost its occupant, he could smell her presence as if she were still there, so recently had she been so. He sighed, staring at the meal he had brought, his stomach gurgling with hunger. Still, he waited, wanting to share it with her and let her have first choice.

"Well, Li, now that Ling is no more..." a voice began, a voice he recognized immediately.

"No more am I?" Ling asked.

Bruno, for it was none other than he, started. "What are you... where is Li?"

Ling shrugged. "I don't know. Now, why did you think I was no more?" Than it occurred to him. "So, Pug was meant to catch me, was he? What happened, Snitch didn't quite alert him fast enough?"

Bruno's cruel red eyes glistened for a moment in anger, then faded to mere cunning. "Why, Ling my friend, I don't know what you mean. I merely heard a rumor that he might have caught you, and I came to comfort poor Li. But now, seeing that you are well, I am delighted not to have to."

Ling frowned. He had long suspected that Bruno had rid himself of anyone who stood in the way of his power by having

Snitch and Pug work together to give the rat catching dog an advantage. Too many of the Chinese rats had disappeared that way. Now, most of those left were Bruno's band, or Saraj's smaller group from India.

"I have brought her dinner," he said simply.

Bruno nodded, staring at the fish head. "I see that. You have been to your otter friends, I take it. How are they?"

Ling had decided as he made his way her with the fish head not to tell Bruno of their story about the petrel. He knew Bruno wanted to get to China, to try his hand with his group at one of the vast cities there where a rat could do well.

"They are fine," Ling said.

Just then, Li appeared at the doorway. She scowled when she saw Bruno, but then her eyes alighted upon Ling and she rushed to him flinging her arms around him and hugging him with all her might. "They said Pug had caught you," she sniffed, tears of joy and relief flowing from her eyes.

"Who said?" He asked gently, running a loving hand over the fur on her head.

"His people," she answered, gesturing at Bruno without looking at him.

Bruno laughed, but not a nice laugh. "Ah," he purred, "you see how rumors make us say ugly things. My people? Are we not one people, we rats? But, I will leave you two now, for I am but a servant of *our* people, and I have work to do." And he left.

Li shuddered, still holding tightly to Ling. "I do not like him at all."

"Nor I," he smiled. "Come, I have brought dinner." He gestured at the fish head.

She pushed herself away from him, wiping her eyes and sniffling. "I smelled it. Is it from the otters?"

"Yes. Our friends, as Bruno accused us. They are our friends, and I have news to share with you about them. But first, let's eat."

Meanwhile, Bruno had found some of the rats in a mixed group, his band and the India rats together, divvying up food brought from the cargo hold. It was not nearly as good as

Ling's fish head, but Bruno waited to mention that until Saraj showed up. He needed his rival to be on board with his own plans. Briskly Bruno took charge in dividing up the food, making certain not to show favoritism to his own group, not here, not now.

While he watched in satisfaction as the rats devoured their food, he felt a slight pull at his tail. He whirled, teeth bared for biting. Snitch stood behind him, head down, submissive.

"What is it?" He demanded, voice low.

"News you will want to hear."

Glancing back to see that all was well here, he motioned for Snitch to follow him. The smaller rat, white-furred with bands of black and a gray tail that had been bitten many times so it was as ragged as the ripped apart ears of the groveling underling, followed him silently. They made their way to a narrow opening between support beams. Here, no one would hear them.

"Tell me your news," Bruno commanded.

"It concerns this ship, and the otters, and perhaps others," Snitch began.

"Yes, yes, what of it?"

But the other rat had news, important news, and he meant to gain something from it. "It also involves, I believe, a traitor in our midst."

Bruno's beady red eyes glowed now. His claws stretched out reflexively, as if to tear the traitor's throat apart. "Who?'

"I have my eyes on a mate," Snitch went on, his agenda clear.

The humorless leader's eyes narrowed. "Who did you have in mind?"

"Li," he answered, saliva leaving his lips as he thought of her sleek fur and bright eyes.

"But she is Ling's," Bruno said.

Snitch now met the gaze of the his leader, "She is too good for a traitor."

Now interest sparkled in Bruno's eyes. "Tell me all of it."

Snitch relayed what he had heard in Meeka's quarters, and added his own suspicions about Ling. Bruno nodded in satisfaction. "If it is true, or even if it is not," he smiled, "we will have Pug take care of Ling. He is the last of the Chinese riff-raff that I had planned to eliminate. But," his eyes glowed, "I'm afraid you will be in for disappointment about the fair Li."

Snitch's head jerked up. "Why? Have I not earned her with all I have done for you?"

"Perhaps," Bruno agreed, "but still, you must pick another. Any other, I will make sure she is yours."

"But why not Li?" Snitch whined.

"Because," the rat snarled, "she is mine!"

"Are they really going to kill the otters when we return?" Li asked, eyes wide with astonishment at all Ling had told her.

He nodded solemnly. "Yes. But I will be dead long before that if Bruno has his way." He shared his suspicions with her about Snitch and Pug.

She didn't act surprised. "I hate Snitch, and I don't trust Bruno a bit either. And the way he looks at me," she shuddered, "so you're going to help them, Ling?'

"Yes, if I can."

She bit her lip, pondering it. "Wrecking the ship. How can it be done?"

Ling

Ling had been asking himself the same question. For a rat, the ship was a whole city in size. Massive beyond belief, even the thought of controlling its travel was beyond him. How it moved, how the sails worked and the massive rudder, were mysteries he had only a vague notion about. On top of that, there were the humans and the puzzle of what they did on board. The cooks he knew and understood. He'd watched them often enough to think he could cook a whole meal if he had to. There were human passengers from India and Vietnam, Cambodia and Burma. All of them he'd watched, since they tended to leave wonderful crumbs of food around. But they were passengers, and what they did had nothing to do with moving the ship.

He realized suddenly that the only nonhuman onboard who might have the knowledge they would need to move the ship was Pek. It was the same conclusion Meeka and those with her had come to. But the Captain's little dog was a mystery to them all. He had never bothered the rats, but again, why should he? He lived with the Captain in his cabin, ate the most wonderful luxury foods reserved for the master of the ship, and had no reason to pay any mind to such low caste creatures as rats.

Still, Ling decided, perhaps it was time he did pay attention to a rat. Me.

Chapter 6   How hard it will be
to convince Pek

The sun beat down as it does along the Great Barrier Reef. A fleet of ships, some regular junks that anyone in the exotic east would recognize as trade vessels from China, others were clearly Dhows from Persia and India, while still others seemed lesser versions of the junk and could be traced to the nations of indo-China. Than there were the giants, ships so big no one had seen such vessels before in the history of the world. Their white sails were like a sea of clouds as the fleet moved majestically together across the churning seas.

On board one of the ships the busy crew scurried around, seeming like dwarfish men against the mighty size of the deck and sails. They worked hard on the ropes and clambered up and down the rigging to the orders of the officers who strode around busily giving orders. The captain stood impassively watching, sometimes nodding at his first officer, other times calmly giving a command in a crisp tone that carried easily across the wide deck. But if one looked carefully, it could be clearly seen that he cradled in his arms a small, pet dog.

It was Pek, of course, and the little dog couldn't have been happier. He imagined that the orders coming from his captain came from him, relayed by the human. Indeed, if the humans knew how to understand his little yips and growls, they would hear him giving commands. "Avast, up the yardarm, furl that sail," he'd order, even as the captain gave the same orders to the crew in their own tongue. For Pek, for all that he was spoiled and thought much of himself, did know how the ship sailed and which orders were the right ones to give.

For this reason, Sharpe wanted to convince the little dog to help them. But it would not be easy. Because Pek loved the boat as much as his captain did. The idea of wrecking it, even to save his own life, which he would be hard put to believe could ever be in danger, would be something he would not even think of doing. Now Sharpe watched the little dog and his master from the coiled rope on deck he loved to stretch out on. The crew knew Sharpe, knew he loved that rope and so were loathe to use it unless they had to. Today they didn't have to. So Sharpe lay on his rope and watched Pek, and the captain and his crew, trying to plan how to say what he'd need to say.

And then, just as the captain finally reached around and placed his pet on the small silk cushion waiting for him just behind and to the left of the captain's command position, Sharpe remembered something. Back when the ship's crew was being assembled, while the ship was being finished, during the rounding up of appropriate creatures for the ship, all the animals except for Pek had been put together in a waiting area, the dogs in one side in kennels and the otters in the other with piles of branches and twigs. Apparently someone had mistaken them for beavers. The Emperor had sent his son to observe the ship operations, hoping the young man might become interested in the fleet and what it had been doing.

The young emperor-to-be had come, with his followers in tow. The followers had fawned on him as the young man had walked around disdaining to touch anything. He was clearly uncomfortable around all things mariner. Somehow, though, he had become aware of the compound for the animals at the same time he noticed Pek in the arms of the captain.

"Good captain," he said, looking to make sure his followers were all around to notice his cleverness, "why is that one dog left to its own devices why all the others are put in that kennel?"

The captain, who knew of the young man and his disdain for seamen and what they did, faced the young man and calmly looked him in the eye. "He is my personal pet, my lord. Your honorable father gave him to me as a present."

If he had known better, the captain would never have said the last. The snorting of the followers and the frown of the young man, though, certainly told him his comment had not been well received.

"He is one of the animals for your ship, is he not?"

The captain was puzzled by the question. "I suppose so."

"Then he belongs with the others."

The captain shook his head. "But, my lord, your father..."

"Sent me here, don't you agree?"

"Yes, my lord."

"So, you will place the cur with the others. In China there should not be such favoritism, it will cause bad feelings. It is my wish," he ended, glaring at the captain. The captain stared at this young upstart emperor-to-be who spoke of favoritism while being fawned upon by a retinue of useless followers. But then, deciding that any disagreement on his part would only result in his losing his command, he had merely nodded and let his pet be taken from his arms.

And so Pek had spent the time leading up to the ship being loaded up with the working animals. Of course, the first thing the captain had done was to bring the animals onboard and rescue his beloved pet. But the time Pek spent in the kennel had given the other dogs a chance to grow to hate the little Pekingese, who had shown his disdain for them and been protected by a seaman sent by the captain to watch over his little favorite. All the dogs that is except Sharpe, who had done his best to keep Pek from being chewed alive by Chow and Bok when the seaman was otherwise preoccupied. While it hadn't been in the little dog's nature to be overly grateful in so many words, yet Pek had a soft spot in his heart whenever he saw Sharpe come around.

Pek

Now Sharpe rose from his coil of rope and slowly made his way over to the little dog. He waited while Pek snuffed at and shuffled the cushion until he had it just the way he wanted it. Not until he was settled gnawing at a bone he had left there did he notice Sharpe watching him.

"Did you see me give orders today?" Pek asked, pleased with himself.

"You had the crew jumping," Sharpe answered, keeping his face serious. It was a game he played with the little dog, letting Pek believe he was the captain of the ship.

"As always."

"The old Emperor would be proud."

Pek was puzzled. "Our Emperor *will* be proud," he corrected.

Sharpe shook his head sadly. "He has gone to his honorable ancestors, Pek. The arrogant son is now our Emperor."

Glaring at Sharpe, the little dog growled. "Impossible. And even if it is possible, how would you know such a thing?"

"The otters. They spoke with a petrel who heard from a bird of the court. The young man is not only emperor now, but he plans to do away with the fleet, and us."

The little dog cocked his head, considered what Sharpe had told him, then snorted in derision. "Otters? A petrel who heard from a court bird? Sharpe, this is nonsense. You could not possibly know such a thing."

Sharpe frowned. He tried again. "You see, while the otters were fishing, the petrel came…"

Pek interrupted him. "Do you hear yourself, Sharpe? Otters are unreliable, always cavorting and playing. They were tricking you, and see, it has worked. Probably even now they are laughing at you." He returned happily to the marrow of the bone he had gnawed into, sucking on it and pleased with himself for setting his friend straight.

Sharpe knew Pek. He could see the pleased expression he wore and knew no further arguments on his part would do. He went back to his rope coil and thought hard. Sharpe usually didn't do any deep thinking, he wasn't that sort. Now he pondered it, though, and tried and tried to find an answer. The otters…no, Pek would not believe them, he'd made that clear. The petrel… wait, that was it. His head rose in pleasure at the thought. If they could bring the petrel to Pek, perhaps he would listen to the bird. He sighed, scratched behind one ear with a hind paw and settled to waiting until he could talk to the otters once again.

The sun felt warm and good, Sharpe was about to relax into a nap when he heard the click-click of nailed paws he recognized. His nose confirmed it. He rose to meet Chow and Bok coming towards him. They growled at Pek but were ignored by the little dog. As long as his captain was near, Pek knew he needn't fear them.

"It seems you have been with your friends the otters lately," Chow growled at Sharpe.

"Useless players," Bok grumbled about them.

Sharpe considered this. He had been with Meeka when the otters came in. She would not have mentioned it to Chow, nor was Chow likely to visit her and get in conversation. He considered her a worthless plant eater. The otters regarded Chow the way he them, as opposites who had nothing in common. That left only one source.

"You seem to work with the rats more than hunt them," Sharpe charged.

Bok's ears went back, but Chow only barked a laugh. "We use them, if that is what you mean. And yes, if that's what you meant, I did hear it from them. What of it? It's the truth, is it not?"

Sharpe lay back on his rope, but his muscles remained tense for danger. "Who my friends are is of no concern to you, Chow," he said.

"Dogs should stay with dogs," Chow growled in answer.

"Dogs like you? I'd rather not."

Bok grunted and pointed his nose at Pek, "No, you'd rather hang around worthless parasites like that one."

Pek growled low, but continued to worry his bone. Answering Bok would be admitting the dog meant something, and he would not do that.

Sharpe sighed. "Every creature has worth, Bok. Even you."

Lips curling up, Bok's fangs came out in a snarl. "Would you like to see what my worth is, you wrinkled piece of trash?"

"I've fought better than you, Bok, and won," Sharpe answered calmly, "and your friend Chow knows it."

Chow's eyes glared at Sharpe, who met that gaze and returned it with the truth of his own words behind him. The lion-maned dog lowered his own eyes and growled at Bok, "Let's go. This serves no purpose. We will be watching you," he remarked as he left, "for disloyalty." Then he left.

Pek's curiosity had been aroused. He regarded his friend with interest. "When we were in the kennels, I wondered why Chow would not fight you. Tell me, friend Sharpe, what story is this you have kept from me?"

Embarrassed, Sharpe considered not telling Pek, but he knew the little dog would not leave him alone until he heard. Besides, perhaps it would help make Pek listen later when they needed him to. He snorted and licked at his front paws.

"Chow and I were once part of the Emperor's royal hunting dogs. We lived in the forest that was part of the Forbidden City. Once, we were taken out with others to hunt for wild boar. The Emperor himself came, but he is old so was carried in a litter with retainers. The boars we came upon all ran, except for one. It charged at the Emperor's litter. His servants who carried it ran, dropping it. The guards threw their spears, but the boar was fast and they missed. Then Chow leapt upon the boar's neck." In Sharpe's mind he could see it, even now, and smell the sweat of fear from the men, the wild rage of the boar, the mad anger of Chow.

"What happened?" Pek demanded, for Sharpe had stopped, lost for a moment in memory.

"Oh," he started, "not much. The boar threw Chow off of him, then ran at him to tear him apart with his tusks. And I came then and bit the boar's neck, killing him." Pek snuffed in amazement. "Just like that? One bite and dead?"

"Well, no. Perhaps I had to fight him some before I could finally get to his neck."

Now Pek understood about Chow. "He hates you because you saved him, because he needed saving. And you did what he could not. You saved the Emperor, too, Sharpe. No wonder Chow is like he is around you. Be careful, my friend. He will not rest until he can find a way to take his shame away."

Sharpe shook his head. "He is all talk."

But Pek disagreed. "He is dangerous. And Bok is worse. Bok will do what Chow orders him to do. Your life is in danger, Sharpe. Be careful."

Chapter 7   An Unexpected Development

Ling's heart pounded in his chest. He had made his way to the crew's mess, on the alert for Pug but confidant he would hear or smell the little rat catcher before he was in danger. Somehow, though, he couldn't get over the feeling someone was following him. He had halted several times and listened when he'd thought he'd heard steps behind him, but if there was someone, whoever it was had always halted just when he did.

"Could be your imagination, Ling," he'd told himself.

In the mess hall the crew had just finished a shift. There were so many on this large junk that they ate with their watch groups, four hours on and four off. Cleanup would begin not long after a group ate, but not immediately, which gave a rat time to scurry in and get what had landed on the floors. The men generally ate noisily, sometimes arguing and flinging rice and vegetables, or even a chunk of meat, to settle a disagreement so there were generally good things to find.

Looking left and right, listening carefully, Ling spied a glob of food under a table halfway across the room. He planned how to get to it, behind sitting benches, under and around tables, always with cover from being seen. He sniffed, but the aroma of the food hung so strong in the air he could not be sure what else might be around. He decided to chance it.

He scurried from cover to cover, each time stopping along the way to sniff and watch. The cooks and the cleanup boys never noticed him, as he intended. Soon he stood over the food, scooping it into his pack. Just finishing and turning to go, he heard the sound.

"Clik-clik."

Instinctively he crouched behind a table leg, scanning the room. The sound had come, from his right. Ling peered around the leg, and saw him. Pug, sniffing the air while advancing towards him, his nails tapping against the wooden floor rhythmically. Then Pug paused, nose uplifted, his head swung with a snap in Ling's direction and he began to run. The doorway lay behind him. Ling turned to run towards the kitchen.

Pug began to bark loudly. The cook and his helpers appeared, saw the rat, disappeared into the kitchen and reappeared with weapons in hand. The two helpers Ling noticed had brooms, but the cook carried a wickedly large butcher knife. The rat ran towards a helper, waited until he was close and the helper had frantically swung the broom, then leaped onto its handle, running up it and then diving over behind the man on into the kitchen itself.

Immediately he was sorry. The only exit was a closed door, the one he'd just come through. There were pots and pans everywhere, bags of rice and other foods, but nothing he could hide in that Pug wouldn't smell him in and find him in an instant. Frantically he ran along the walls, hoping to find an opening, a crack, a knothole, anything. He was scratching at a weak looking wooden plank when Pug scurried in.

"End of the line, Ling," Pug growled. "I'll make it quick, though, one snap of your neck and that'll be it."

Ling wheeled, still hoping to find an opening somewhere. "So kind of you," he answered, hoping to keep Pug talking.

Pug gave a small smile. "Always had a weak spot for you, Ling. You're a worthy opponent. I might even save your tail to remember you by." His small sharp teeth grinned whitely.

"Not like you'd do to Snitch, huh? He just tells you where to find us. Catching him would be too easy, and he's too useful."

The little dog reared his head back, growling. "What do you know about it?'

"Only that you have a deal with Bruno and he's been leading you to most of the Chinese rats on board. The Italian and Indian rats now outnumber us greatly. Not very patriotic of you."

Pug snuffled and shook his head. "My job is to catch rats. Doesn't matter which ones. Bruno and Snitch just made it easier. Someday I'll get him, too. For now he's useful."

Before he could say more, the cook rushed in, eyes wild and wide, moving his head back and forth looking for Ling. When he saw the rat, he threw the wicked butcher knife in his hand. It thunked into the wood just inches from the rat who leaped high, hurriedly scrambling up onto the work table. One of the helpers rushed up with his broom to sweep Ling onto the floor and the waiting rat catcher below. Ling saw him and prepared to dodge the broom.

Unfortunately, he had forgotten there were two helpers. While his eyes were fixed on the one, he suddenly felt the other broom smash against his back and send him hurtling off the table to the floor below. Pug dashed at him as he fell. He knew the little dog's teeth were moments from his neck and death.

Then a large, brown form came lunging into the room, shoving Pug aside at the last moment, grabbing Ling in powerful jaws and running as quickly as it had arrived out of the kitchen. In moments the dog had disappeared, leaving relieved kitchen workers and a very confused Pug in his wake.

Minutes later they were down deep in the hold of the ship, in Meeka's quarters, and Sharpe released Ling, unharmed, from his mouth. He went to get a drink of water from a bucket left for Meeka. Ling collapsed, the terror of the last few minutes making him shaky and scarcely able to think.

"Why..." he gasped, felt his heart still beating wildly, took two deep breaths and tried again. "Why did you save me?"

"We asked him to," a voice behind him spoke.

Ling whirled. Yong and Bao, as well as Hui. She was the one who had spoken. Ling remembered she seemed to be the leader of the Otters. Now she came over to him and smiled.

"Are you sorry we did?"

Ling laughed. "Sorry to be alive? No. I'm very grateful, but also very curious. Why did you?"

"We need you, that's the first reason. The other is that we like you and we found out that Snitch followed you to lead Pug to you."

"How did you find out?"

"I overheard Snitch talking to Pug when I went to see him," Sharpe said, licking his lips as water dripped from his chin. "So I came to tell Yong, and Hui told me to hurry to the mess hall and save you. So I did."

He sat and licked his paws clean.

Digesting this, Ling found he was grateful, and more curious than ever. "I'm glad you need me. What do you need me for?"

Hui filled Ling in on what Sharpe had tried to do with Pek. Ling hadn't had contact with the Captain's little dog, but he'd heard the gossip of the other rats. The scraps Pek received for his dinner were from the Captain's table, and were the best food on board ship. Once or twice rats had been brave enough to try and steal some. One had succeeded. He had had bragging rights for some time, but Ling had noticed he never went again.

"So, if we can convince Pek, he could help us sail the ship?" Ling asked.

Bao shrugged and looked at Yong. He sighed. "He can tell us what to do, but we aren't sure we can do it. We're animals, not humans. We've never sailed. Still, it's our only chance."

"If you can convince Pek to help."

"Yes."

Ling realized suddenly where this was going. "He won't believe you, but he might believe the bird, right?"

Sharpe grunted. Hui spoke up. "Ling, we hope the next time the otters are allowed to hunt, or even swim, Stormy will still be out there and we can find him. Then we will need to convince him to fly up to Pek when he's on deck and tell him. And then we hope he'll believe the petrel. But we're afraid he will fly away before we next are let outside to swim. You, Ling, are our next hope. We think we can get you on deck and have you look for him. If you can get Stormy to come close, you can explain what we need."

"It's dangerous on deck for me," Ling told them. He knew he'd try, but he wanted them to know this.

"We know, friend Ling," Bao's face was creased in concern, "and we won't blame you if you decide not to. But soon we're afraid the fleet will sail for China. Once we're out to sea, we may not have another chance. And once we return home all the animals will be killed." Her sweet face spoke gravely, but calmly.

"We also think it will be not so dangerous for you if Sharpe takes you on deck at night. Then you can clamber up the ropes and hide until day. If you have another plan," Hui explained, "we'll gladly try that."

"No, your plan sounds good. I just wish..." he paused.

"What?" Bao asked.

"Li will be worried that I have not returned. And Bruno," he grew angry just thinking of the rat who had tried to have him killed, "will come to her and...can you get word to her?"

The otters could not meet his gaze. They wanted him to help, and also wanted to help him. Sharpe could not come anywhere near the rat's lair, even if he could fit. The rats would attack or run, but they wouldn't talk to the dog. The otters couldn't leave the hold. If they tried they would be stopped. They were all too big to fit in the tunnels that Ling and Snitch had taken.

"It's all right," Ling said, "I understand. The tunnel to our lair is too small for any of you..."

"Wait," Hui suddenly spoke up, "what about Pipi?"

Yong understood her immediately. "Yes, Pipi is small enough to fit in the tunnel, if he squeezes. But will Huang and Yan let him go?"

"They must, or Ling's friend is in danger, true?" Hui asked. Ling nodded, reluctantly. "Wait here, friend Ling, while we find out."

As they began to leave, Ling remembered something. "Wait. Pipi is the pup, right?"

They turned. 'Yes."

"Bruno is dangerous. It isn't safe for him. Look, let me just go. I can find Li and be right back."

"You cannot go back, friend Ling," Hui told him solemnly. "Snitch was heard to say that Bruno has declared they will kill you themselves if this does not work. They are looking for you, waiting for you by now. Snitch no doubt has told Bruno by now."

Ling's eyes flared with anger. He wasn't afraid of Bruno, "All the more reason I need to get Li out and to safety."

Hui sighed and said, "If you die, where is safety? We need you, and risking your life here might end ours. Don't underestimate otters. Even a pup might surprise you." And they left.

Sharpe closed his eyes and began to nap. Ling stirred impatiently, wondering how this would go. He wanted to get word to Li, to get her safely down here, but he worried for the otter pup. The rats could kill him if Bruno ordered it. Then a noise came from behind him.

"Do not worry. Even the pups of otters must be resilient," a voice said, "if these otters are any indication."

He turned to see Meeka. He'd known about the giant sloth, but they had never met. Now it occurred to him that she had been there the whole time, listening silently. "You were quiet through all of that. Why?"

Meeka smiled. "Before now I had nothing to say. Now I want to tell you something Ling. If you can help the otters, you will not only be saving their lives. You will be saving mine, too."

"Yours?" And then it hit him. "All the animals are to die," he spoke aloud what he'd heard.

"I'm sorry. We rats are used to being hunted and killed, but you, it isn't right. They captured you, you didn't come aboard by choice."

Meeka sighed. "I have come to understand that I will never see my home again, or my friends. But I have new friends now, and I wish to live. So, if we can find a way to get to land, I will live there."

"Life is a lamp-flame before a wind," a voice spoke softly. Ling and Meeka both gave startled sounds, hers a grunt, his a small squeak. Sharpe merely opened one eye, sniffed and then closed it again, snoring softly. A small dog came out of the shadows. It was Shih.

"Tell me about the danger," he commanded.

Ling eyed him. The little dog was the most unpredictable of the animals on board ship. As a Buddhist, he had never been known to kill a rat. Still, he was a dog, and the rats all knew he could if he wanted to. His strange sayings made no sense most of the time, and he seemed not to need friends, and yet he always found a way to be around Pek or Sharpe or Chow. The only one he never seemed to be around was Bok. Bok no one but Chow hung around. The crew fed Shih and seemed to almost revere him, but no one ever picked him up as the Captain did Pek, or stroked his fur as they did Sharpe.

"Sharpe, why did you not warn us he was here?" Ling asked.

Sharpe, without stirring or opening an eye, answered, "He might be of help. He won't harm you, will you, Shih?"

"No," Shih answered. "All the animals will die, you said. Tell me why."

"Perhaps you had better hear it from the otters," Ling said, "I only know what they told me."

"So," a voice behind, the otter Yong it turned out to be, made Ling whirl, "the priest now knows some things. We did not tell you before, because we thought you would tell Chow. Why should we now tell you?"

Ling had been trying to figure out how these animals could appear around him without his nose warning him first. He realized it was Meeka. Her odor was strong, and foreign, and confused his sense of smell. He watched as behind Yong came Zan and Huang, the parents, leading the little pup, Pipi. The little otter seemed excited, frisking and running in and out of the legs of his parents.

"Friend Ling," Pipi ran to the rat, "you must tell me how to go, and what to watch for, and everything." He moved around Ling, back and forth as he talked. It was dizzying.

Zan had followed his son and stood nearby. "Tell him especially what to be careful of, how to stay away from Bruno and trouble," he requested.

"And how to get back," Huang added, standing behind Zan.

"Take him to the tunnel opening and tell him everything," Bao commanded, coming behind the parents, "We will be explaining things to Master Shih."

Ling did as he was told. He hoped the pup was listening, because he never seemed to be still and it was hard to tell. His parents did not seem to think his behavior was odd, so Ling tried hard to concentrate on details, how to make his way, what to watch for, how not to be seen, all the time wishing it was he going and not the little pup. He explained the back way into Li's, a way even Bruno did not know about, he hoped. He made Pipi repeat it back to him. "Do you have any questions?"

Pipi nodded. "How will I make her believe me? I mean, she won't just come, will she? How will she know it was really you who sent me, and not a trick of some kind?"

It was a surprisingly good question, one that hadn't even occurred to Ling. He began to respect the little otter more. "Tell her that the one who brought her Jasmine tea in the garden asks her to trust you."

"Jasmine tea in the garden," Pipi repeated. "Okay. Now I'll go. See everyone soon."

"Be careful," Huang ordered, hugging her son. Zan patted him on the head and nodded. In a flash, the little pup was gone up the hole of the tunnel, out of sight.

They returned to where the others had been talking to Shih. Ling noticed the little dog's face had become graver than usual. He seemed to be nodding at Yong. Ling heard him say, "You are right. Only the bird might convince Pek. He loves this ship and his Captain. Getting him to help crash it...even the bird might not be enough."

"Let us hope it is," Yong said to him, "because he is our only hope. None of the rest of us knows anything about handling this ship."

Shih pondered what he had heard. Like the other dogs, he had been unimpressed with the young prince when he had come to inspect the ship. What he had done to Pek had struck Shih as petty, a sign of a very mean spirit. In the next life he hoped the young man would be something small and defenseless. Then he chided himself inside for such thoughts. Still, things should balance. He spoke to all of them. "Well, than let us hope all our efforts can convince Pek. Having met this young Emperor, I believe you, and I do not wish for any of you to die."

They all nodded agreement to that.

"Now I will go ponder the way of things," Shih told them, "while you await the fate of the pup and the mate."

He left. The others watched him go, wondering what it meant for this mysterious dog to know so much.

Chapter 8   The Courage of the Young

For Pipi it was a wonderful adventure. He had spent his entire life in the hold. As an otter, that had been horrible. Otters need to swim and have adventures. His little soul had nearly shriveled without those things. Only the love and care of his parents and the playful attention of all the others had made it endurable. That, plus the many times he had snuck away to see Meeka who had let him swim in her watering trough.

"I wish we could all get out of this ship and live like otters should," he'd once said to her.

She'd smiled lovingly at the little otter, "And what would you do 'living like an otter should?' Tell me."

Happily, he did. He'd heard his parents and the others talk time and again of their lives before, of the slides down minor waterfalls where streams fed into high-cliffed ocean, or cavorting among the rocky shores chasing each other and playing tag. "First I'd find a cliff to dive off of into the water," he told her, "then I'd chase fish and maybe seals."

His parents had warned him about seals, that they liked to play as much as the otters but were bigger and played rough. But Yong, who was his hero, had scoffed. "They're not so rough. And they're not faster than an otter. Many is the time I've played nip and tag with them and outraced even their fastest."

Pipi recalled all of this as he made his way, following Ling's directions, towards the rats' homes. He was enjoying himself immensely, and wished he had someone along to yip and wrestle with. The smells around him nearly assaulted his nostrils with so many new and different odors. Living in the small part of the hold given to the otters his entire young life he had known so few. Then he smelled strongly the odor he identified with Ling. Rat. He knew he was close. It was not fear, though, that made his young heart beat stronger. It was excitement.

"You will not be seeing our friend Ling again, I'm afraid," Bruno told Li, eyeing the female rat with greedy eyes. "So, you had best come with me. I can protect you and provide much better food than you have ever known."

Li was crying softly. "You say Snitch saw Pug kill Ling?"

"Yes. Very tragic. He fought bravely Snitch said."

She glanced at the rat, her tears drying suddenly. His voice...he lied. She knew this without knowing how she knew. Everything within her had protested at the news of Ling's death, and now she knew why. *He's alive, I know it. Every fiber of my being says so.* She straightened and pointed a finger at Bruno. "Please leave my home," she told him.

He stiffened. "That is not wise, Li. You need a protector. There are other rats who would not treat you as well as I will."

"I am Ling's," she answered. "And I will be here when he comes for me."

Bruno snorted derisively, "He's dead, I tell you. He won't ever come back."

"You lie," she trembled as she said it, "and I wish you to leave, now."

Taking a step towards her, the brown rat's eyes glowed with desire and a sense of power. "I could take you now," he said.

She snarled and bared her teeth, her trembling still there but rage making her fearless, "Not alive. And I will die fighting dearly. Are you ready for that?"

He hadn't been prepared for that. Deep inside, Bruno, like most bullies, was a coward. He stepped back before her anger.

"You wait," he sneered, "when Snitch comes to take you, you'll beg for me." Then he turned and left.

Li collapsed then to the floor, sobbing.

"Don't cry," a small voice behind her brought her to her feet in astonishment.

There stood a creature...an otter pup, she realized. "How did you...only Ling knew of that secret way...who are you?"

"My name is Pipi," he said. He smiled and came a little way further. The room was small for him, he had barely squeezed around many of the corners of the tunnel he had taken to come here. "Ling has sent me to get you."

"Ling?" She frowned. She wanted to believe him, but Bruno had made her suspicious. "How do I know this isn't a trick?"

His pup face wrinkled in thought, making him cute and guileless. How could he be part of anything from Bruno? she thought. Still, the cruel rat had shaken her to the core. She didn't know what to believe.

"Oh, now I remember," Pipi yipped. "He said, tell her the one who gave you Jasmine tea in the garden sent me."

She smiled at the memory. Ling and the tea, no one else on board ship would know of that. "You are from Ling," she smiled. "Where are we going? Where is Ling?"

"With my family and our friends."

Suddenly a rat came in unannounced. It was Snitch, and for a moment he didn't see Pipi. "Bruno said if I could make you come with me, I could have you," he swaggered, grabbing Li by the front paw. She struggled.

"Let go of me."

Pipi didn't even think, he just slammed into the rat the way any otter would in play, the only way Pipi knew. Otters don't know their own strength. Snitch was thrown clear across the room and slammed into the wall, collapsing unconscious. Li stood unharmed in the middle of the room where he had grabbed her.

"Come on," Pipi said, "we need to go."

She surveyed her home quickly, knowing everything left would be lost. What did she need, what would Ling need? She realized there was nothing. In all their time on this ship, they had accumulated bits of this and that, but not a thing that either of them would miss.

"All right," she told the pup, "let's go."

Pipi nodded, eager to be gone. The smell of danger, of terror from Li, of greed, cunning and cruelty from Snitch made his nose twitch and his stomach turn over. He wanted nothing more than to be away from this place. Snitch lay unmoving, though he was clearly breathing. This confused Pipi. He'd barely nudged him, he thought, why didn't he move? It all was too much. He was suddenly tired of the adventure. I'll get this female to Ling, and then be back with my mother, father and the others.

Leading the way, he tried to hurry, but found the corners where he had to squeeze himself through frustrating. Li tried to help, pushing him when he became momentarily stuck. For her, fear dogged her steps. She imagined Bruno leading a pack of rats behind them, his greedy red eyes aflame with anger and hatred. "Hurry, hurry," she kept saying, quietly but insistently. The little pup tried his best.

They were halfway to the hold when she heard it. The frantic scratching of a horde of rat feet on wood. The chase was on, and it was not merely Bruno or Snitch. It was a pack of rats. The sound had been distant when she'd first heard it, but as the minutes passed and poor Pipi kept being delayed by tight corners, Li could hear the pack coming closer and closer. Before she knew it, she could smell them. Then she heard Bruno's voice.

"Give up now, Li, or we'll kill the otter pup."

She stopped. Pipi noticed and tried to turn around in the narrow passage. "Why are you stopping?"

"Go back," she told the pup. "Tell Li we tried."

Pipi had heard Bruno's voice. At first, the words had filled him with fear. But then he had remembered Yong and the way he had saved the others from the white killer. Yong was his hero. He couldn't return and say he had failed because he was afraid.

Li prepared to be captured by Bruno. She closed her eyes, dreading the fate that awaited her. Oh, Ling, she thought, I'm so sorry. Then she felt herself being picked up. Had they come already?

"Go to Ling," Pipi's voice said.

She opened her eyes. The young otter was in front of her, facing the oncoming rats. 'No," she protested. "What did you do?"

"I put you behind me," he told her. "My friend Ling counted on me bringing you back. And my family," here Pipi's voice choked a moment as he thought of his parents and the other otters. Would he ever see them again? "My family chose me to come. We otters are noble," he added that, it was something he had decided on his own, "and we do not let others down."

Li heard the rats approaching, saw the little pup bravely facing them. She sobbed. "I cannot leave you here alone to face them."

His voice came, calmly now, ready for his fate. "You must, Li. Otherwise what I do now will be for nothing. Go, and remember the courage of otters."

She gulped, realizing the young pup was right. If, after they were done with him, they found her waiting behind him, all that he had done would have been for nothing. With terror in her heart for Pipi she turned and ran for the ship's hold.

Chapter 9   No honor among villains

When Li arrived in the hold the otters were waiting, breathlessly. Their little pup held a dear place in all their hearts. As Li entered the hold, everyone breathed a sigh of relief. Ling rushed to take her in his arms, but she pushed him away.

"What is wrong?" He asked.

Huang had been staring at the opening Li had come out of, waiting to see her pup. She could not smell him. She sniffed at the opening, calling softly, "Pipi?"

Now she turned to Li. "Where is Pipi?"

Li began to sob. The otters gathered around her, peppering her with questions. Ling stood helplessly, not knowing what to do. A calm voice stopped them all.

"Be quiet, everyone. Can't you see how upset she is?"

It was Meeka. The giant sloth lumbered over, reaching down a giant paw to gently pat Li on her head. "There, there dear. Take deep breaths. You're with friends now." She waited while Li did as she asked. When the female rat seemed composed enough, Meeka said, "Now, Li, tell us where Pipi is."

Looking helplessly at the otters, than at Ling, she said, "I'm not sure. The rats found us in the tunnel, Bruno and a horde of his gang," she said to Ling, who nodded, "and then Pipi put me behind him and told me to come here. That whatever happened to him, if I didn't come it would all be for nothing." She began to cry again just thinking of it.

Huang screamed and fainted. Zan ran to her. Bao stared at them, then at Yong. "What can we do?"

Yong turned to Ling, but the rat was already disappearing down the hole. Yong ran to it and cried, "Ling, where are you going?"

"To find Pipi," his voice answered, "this is my fault."

When Pipi's attackers first came upon him in the narrow tunnel, they hesitated. They would have to come upon him one at a time where he was, two at the most, and though he was only an otter pup, still he was an otter with strong claws on his paws and a ready bite to his teeth. Bruno yelled to the rats to charge the otter. "Hurry. We must finish him off before Li gets away."

"You said a villain had grabbed her and we had to rescue her," Saraj's voice was angry. "We came to save her, but all along she was rushing away? This smells, Bruno."

Bruno snarled, "This is the villain right in front of you. Li will get lost, I meant. We need to find her before that happens."

Pipi had listened, and now he saw that Saraj might be a friend. "She was escaping from Bruno," he said, "I was taking her to Ling, because Bruno tried to kill Ling." Saraj approached the otter to hear more.

"He's an otter!" Bruno cried. "They all lie. Kill him, quickly."

"You come get me yourself, big mouth," Pipi challenged the rat. "I'll teach you to call otters names."

Saraj had never fully trusted Bruno. His rats had worked with Bruno's because it seemed best with the dogs killing so many. But he had long suspected something wasn't quite right about that. Too many of the rats Pug had killed had been Chinese for it to be pure chance. He'd watched Bruno and Snitch carefully for some time now. He wondered just where Snitch went each time Bruno sent him.

"I would like to hear what this pup has to say," Saraj told Bruno.

"And I would not," Bruno snarled. He motioned to two of his rats. "Kill him first," he ordered, motioning to Saraj. They advanced on the surprised rat. Saraj's rats were caught by surprise. He would have been killed if Pipi hadn't been paying close attention. With the speed only an otter could have, he lunged forward and pulled Saraj out of danger and put him behind him. The attacking rats found themselves facing a smiling otter pup who batted them with swift paws and sent them reeling back to Bruno.

Saraj's rats by then had recovered from the shock of Bruno's order. They rushed to save their leader. Soon rats were snarling and fighting each other in the crowded tunnel, paying no attention to Pipi. Saraj, meanwhile, was frantically tapping at the otter.

"Let me get by you and help my friends," he said.

Pipi did as he asked. In moments Saraj had gotten his troops in order. They faced Bruno's rats in a tight circle down the tunnel where it widened, ready to fight and protect each other as they did so. Bruno could see that he could not win this fight. He howled with rage, then shook a fist at Saraj.   "This is not over. Beware of Pug, traitor, you and your rats. We will get revenge. Perhaps on your families." With that parting shot, he and his cronies ran back to the rat lair.

Saraj, startled by the threat, yelled to his rats, "Back to the lair, we must protect our families."

In moments, Pipi found himself alone.

He was headed back down the tunnel to the hold when Ling found him. The rat nearly ran up Pipi's face he had been hurrying so, and he fell back, panting and breathing hard, staring up at the otter pup.

"Pipi. Are you all right?"

Pipi smiled. This had been a grand adventure. "I'm great friend Ling," he said, "but I'm very tired of being in this tunnel. Can we hurry back down?"

In moments they were popping out the tunnel hole into the hold and the surprised arms of their friends and family. Huang and Zan engulfed the little pup with hugs and kisses, while Li cried with joy and hugged Ling. Yong and Bao watched with Meeka, while Hui waited patiently to find out what had happened. It took some time, but finally she made Huang and Zan release their pup so he could tell his story.

Ling listened in wonder as Pipi told of the treachery to Saraj. "I have waited for this," he told them all, "Bruno has stepped too far, finally. Saraj is a rat with honor. Perhaps things will turn now for the rats."

Yong approached Pipi and cuffed him playfully. "So, you recalled my adventure with the white killer and faced the rats." He smiled. "Pipi, you are a true otter now."

Huang scowled at Yong. "Oh, wonderful, now if we ever let him swim in the sea he will hunt for white killers. Stop putting ideas in his head, Yong. Come, Zan, we must put him to bed." She leveled Zan with a fierce gaze and hustled them back to the otters' lair. Yong laughed.

"Are we ready now to go on deck?" Sharpe asked. They had forgotten about the dog. He had waited, napping, while all this took place. They saw that Shih had left some time before. Yong hoped the little dog could be trusted, but knew there was nothing they could do about him if he decided to tell Chow.

"Yes," Ling answered.

Li stopped him, grabbing at his forepaw and staring in his eyes, hers wide and frightened. "Where are you off to, now? More danger I'm sure."

Ling sighed. He explained what the others wanted him to do. "I must try to contact the bird," he told her, "but I will be careful, I promise."

"I will show him where to hide in the coils of my rope," Sharpe assured her. "And it is night, so it will hard for anyone to see him."

"Especially a bird," Li noted. "You do not fool me. He will go up at night, but it is the day when he must find the bird, and expose himself to danger."

Yong and Bao felt for her. She had just come from great danger, found her male alive and unharmed, and now must see him go off to possible death. Bao knew how she had felt when the white killer had been chasing Yong. But it was Hui who surprised them with her wisdom.

"You are right to be concerned," Hui came and gently touched Li with a paw. "He will have no one to watch his back as he scans the heavens. Perhaps," she paused, then smiled at Li, "if you went along you could watch out for each other."

"No!" Ling exclaimed immediately. "It is too dangerous for her."

"And not for you?" Hui asked. "Do you not think she die a thousand deaths waiting and worrying down here. Will she not do more, for you, for herself, for all of us, if she is allowed to go with on deck? Do not think that only you males can be brave and save this ship. It will take each of us."

Ling did not know what to say. He had sent them to rescue Li from danger, not to expose her to it. Yet, there was much wisdom in Hui's words. It would take them all, and he had to admit to himself he had worried much about being alone with no one to watch for danger when he would climb high into the sails to find the soaring bird. He looked at Li. She returned his gaze, a calm assurance in her eyes telling him he could not say no. He sighed. "I see that it must be so. For what man can truly order a woman to do what she does not want to do, and still say he loves her? But," he admonished Li as she started to smile, "you will stay by my side and do everything I tell you to do."

She bowed slightly, and almost mockingly, at him. "Of course, Ling. For you are the master of this, and I only the student."

Bao laughed. Yong frowned at her and she stuck out her tongue. In moments they were scampering and wrestling around the hold. The others laughed also, even Meeka, and only Ling remained serious.

He knew Li, and the look in her eye had been one of acceptance of his words, and yet a streak of independence. He hoped it did not mean she would be reckless.

Chapter 10 Illusion is all we have

"You fool," Bruno hissed at Snitch, who cowered in fear, "if you had simply grabbed Li instead of talking to her, none of this would have happened."

"She is not one to simply be grabbed," Snitch whined. "And there was that otter pup. How was I to know he was there?"

"Bah, you're a coward." Bruno did not mention his own cowardice before Li, for Bruno was not the type to ever admit being wrong. He had hurried back to the rats' lair, intending to grab the mates and children of Saraj's group, but the Indian rats had been too quick, arriving just behind them. Bruno and his rats had had to defend their own nests. Now he faced problems bigger than worrying about Ling and Li.

"Those rats will have to eat," Bruno said, "and to eat they will have to scavenge where Pug, Chow and Bok can catch them. You must follow them and alert Pug. I want them dead."

Snitch didn't like this. It had been one thing to follow the Chinese rats when they did not know he was doing so. Even then he had been terrified every time he had to meet with Pug. The rat catcher's gleaming teeth had made him quiver with anxiety and fear each time they talked. But Saraj would be wary. If Snitch were caught by any of his group, he knew death would be quick and unpleasantly painful.

"They will be watching for me," Snitch complained. "They already suspect me."

"So don't get caught," Bruno snapped at him. "You're worthless to me if you can't do this. So, either risk getting caught, or have me break your spine. Your choice," he finished savagely.

Snitch had no misconceptions about his value to Bruno. Still, he thought he had become valuable, had become someone Bruno could confide in, almost a friend. He realized now that Bruno had no friends, wanted none. He shivered. And no one else likes me at all, Snitch thought. In fact, everyone hates me. Still, I live well, have plenty of food, and there will be many mates to choose from once the Indian rats are taken care of. He decided that would be enough for him.

"I will go see Pug, tell him to be ready," Snitch said.

"Good." Bruno dismissed him without a glance.

On deck, Chow and Bok were pacing, barking at the flapping sails and worrying. The two had noticed Sharpe's sudden absences, and Pug seemed disturbed by something, but hadn't shared what it was when Chow demanded to know. Although both dogs enjoyed being on deck for the sunshine and breezes that offered fresh smells, they dreaded running into Pek, who would lord his exalted station as Captain's pet over them. Pek wasn't on deck at present, so the two dogs at least hadn't that to worry about. Yet.

"Something happened with Pug," Chow growled. "We need him to tell us what it was."

Bok grunted. "The little rat catcher is too full of himself. How dare he not answer your questions. I should teach him a lesson."

"Softly," Chow admonished as Bok had begun to bark his anger, "with Pug, that will not work. We need someone else." He paused, then nodded to himself. "Of course, the meditative one. Shih can get him to talk."

"Why would Shih do that for us?"

Chow grinned. "Because we will make him see that he should. He has a great sense of his own importance, Shih does. If we flatter him, he will do it."

"I don't like to flatter."

"I know. That's why you will let me talk to him."

They went below deck, to the kennel area reserved for the dogs. Sure enough, Shih was there, pondering his prayer beads. Chow approached him.

"Good Shih, are you deep in prayer?"

Shih

The beads clicked for several minutes, Shih seeming to not notice the other dogs. Bok shuffled impatiently, but Chow merely waited. Finally the little dog stopped, looked up and sighed. "Sometimes my thoughts are as the wind which is not deep, but is often too high for the things of earth."

Bok growled in disgust. He hated when Shih spoke like that. He never understood the little dog. Chow was undisturbed by it.

"We need your help, Shih, precisely because you have such thoughts."

Shih cocked his head to the side, tongue lazily out. "Why is this?"

"Have you noticed anything about our friend, Pug?" Chow asked.

Shih considered. He had noticed Pug's wish for solitude, how disturbed the little dog seemed. He wondered that Chow had, and decided to find out. "I have. He seems to be wrestling with something in his soul."

"We would like to help him," Chow said, "but we cannot if he will not share what is wrong. Can you find out for us, good Shih?"

So, Shih thought, Pug isn't sharing with them. That was odd. Usually the rat catcher worked hand in glove with these two. I'm very curious now. What could make him not want to share? What secret...something he is troubled about, even embarrassed? Shih knew guessing was no good.

"Of course," Shih told them, "I would be glad to talk to Pug."

"And you'll tell us what you find?" Bok spoke up for the first time.

Chow frowned at his friend. "He means, we would be grateful if we can also know what you find to help our friend."

"Ah, to be a good friend is to obtain good Kharma," Shih said. Then he walked away having made no promises.

He found Pug in the mess hall, a place the little dog often prowled, hoping to catch rats come for food. But where usually Pug would be pacing and sniffing, now he merely lay just to the left of the door, seemingly deep in thought. Shih, without disturbing him, quietly came and sat beside him. He sat patiently, listening to the kitchen crew, smelling the many odors of the room and pondering the ways of the universe.

"I don't need company," he heard Pug growl after a bit.

"The whole universe is company," Shih told him.

'Hmmph."

Shih had been analyzing the smells in the room. Pug was the only dog who came, the others feeling it beneath them to beg for food or engage in rat catching, at least not here where the crew might see them fail. Chow and Bok preferred to catch the rats when Pug chased them to where they were waiting, usually in a secluded part of the ship. Shih knew they didn't like to admit they needed Pug's help and wouldn't let the crew watch Pug do most of the work. So no scent of those two hung in the air, nor of Pek who never came to such a lowly place. But...Sharpe. The big dog's smell hung delicately, as if he had come only briefly. Shih began to put together things from his meeting in Meeka's hold with the otters.

"You have had much success on our voyage catching rats," Shih stated.

Pug stared at him, then growled, "It is my job."

"There is great pride in doing one's job." Shih stared straight ahead. "It can be damaging to the soul to have a job stolen away."

"What do you know about it?"

Shih decided to guess. "You have long wanted to catch Ling. He is a master thief, for a rat."

There was no sound for some time next to him. Shih continued staring ahead, waiting. Finally, with a small barking grunt, Pug said, "He was mine. I had him. He had no right to steal him from me."

"No doubt, no doubt. And yet, our friend Sharpe is no thief. He must have had a very good reason, don't you think?"

Pug now bumped against Shih. "How do you know so much, bead twirler?"

But Shih had decided he knew all he needed to. He sighed. "How do you know so little, Pug? You engage in death so much, you do not see life. Your two friends, Chow and Bok, are no better. Perhaps Sharpe sees what none of us do because he looks for life."

"They are not my friends," Pug snorted.

"It is said that all is illusion," Shih told him, "and yet, illusion is all we have. The illusion you have created has left you alone, Pug. Perhaps you need to create a new one."

He walked away while Pug stared after him, pondering his words.

Snitch found him this way some time later. He approached the little dog cautiously, as always. Pug didn't move as he came as near as he dared, hiding behind a table leg.

"Master Pug?" Snitch asked timidly. Something in the distracted manner of the dog frightened him. Usually Pug moved quickly and restlessly. Now he lay staring and breathing shallowly.

Finally, Pug moved his head to regard Snitch. "So, coward, have you come to betray more of your kind?"

Snitch trembled. The words startled him. He knew it was true, but Pug had never so said before. Besides, he wasn't betraying his own rats, he told himself, just the others. But the thought rang hollow in his head.

"Bruno says we will now give you the Indian rats."

"And when they are gone and it is only you, do you think I will stop catching rats?" Pug asked. "Or do you think you will all be too clever for me?"

This wasn't going well, Snitch thought. Pug's questions were ones he had hidden from himself, afraid to think about. Now they slammed into him like body blows.

"I...I merely bring you word from Bruno..." began Snitch. Pug then moved remarkably fast. Snitch had let his guard down, tricked by the little dog's posture and seeming indifference. Before he could get two steps away, Pug had his backbone in his teeth. Snitch waited to die, trembled with fear as he anticipated the crush of teeth against his bones, the pain of death. But Pug did not crunch.

"You see how easily I could kill you?" Pug spoke quite clearly as he held the rat. Suddenly he let go. Snitch waited, not daring to move. The dog could catch him again before he got a step away. "You and Bruno are slime. You have no sense of honor. Go ahead and tell me when the Indian rats are coming, the way you always do. But remember, in the end I will kill you and Bruno. No one escapes me." He paused then, as if remembering something. "Now go."

Snitch fled then, never looking back until he had scrambled into a hole too small for the dog to get through. He looked back then. Pug had returned to his place by the doorway. He lay, seemingly asleep. Snitch shuddered and made his way back to the rat lair.

Chapter 11   A time to be daring

Ling and Li clung to the folds of skin under Sharpe's belly. The dog, as if nothing unusual were occurring, took his time making his way to his favorite coil of rope. Several sailors stopped to pat his head, while the two rats cringed and waited to be found out, but the dog arched his back and panted happily, and the sailors continued on their way to their duties. Finally Sharpe came to the coil and settled within it while Ling and Li found hiding places inside.

"I thought the sailors would find us out for sure," Li gasped. "Why did you stop and let them pet you?" She demanded of Sharpe.

He grinned. "They find what they expect to find. Since I acted normally, they expected to find nothing. Had I eluded them, which I never do, they might have grown suspicious. Have faith, little one, you are safe are you not?"

Ling spoke up. "For now. And it is night so the lanterns hung around the deck offered the only light. I can see now there was little chance of being found. But still, my heart was in my throat. Do any of the other dogs come on deck? Surely they will smell us."

Sharpe snorted softly, licking a paw eyes closed. "Not at night."

Li saw the moon, a quarter moon, also gave light to the deck. Still, there were long shadows where bulkheads, cargo, masts and other items were scattered around the deck. They should be able to make their way up one of the masts and rest in an observation nest at the top. There they would await the day and look for the bird. Yong had described Stormy in detail to them. Still, both doubted this would work. Why would a bird hang around a ship? The others had been hopeful, or maybe desperate, and the two rats knew they must try.

"We will go now, friend Sharpe," Ling said, motioning Li to follow him.

The wrinkled dog nodded and continued licking his front paws.

They were careful. After each hurried dash from shadowed area to the next such, they would pause, sniff the air, listen closely. The crewmen were easy to stay away from. The men seemed to have regular routines and would work at one area, then move to another and stay until that task was finished. They weren't aware of the rats, nor would they have reason to worry about them. In a short time they had come to the tallest mast on the vessel. With a nod from Ling, Li went up first.

The higher they climbed the more the wind tore at them. Li had thought this would be the easiest part of their adventure, but it was proving to be the hardest, and most dangerous. Gusts of wind tore at her as she tried to cling to the wood with her paws. If it had not been for the many ropes tied to the many stays and beams all the way up, she might well have been taken by a stiff breeze and hurled out into the black waters below. When she finally reached the observation nest near the top and climbed into its sheltering walls, her heart thudded like a beating hammer in her chest and her eyes were wide with fear. Ling joined her moments later. His heart, too, she could tell, beat wildly.

"That was frightening," she told him.

He nodded. "A lot more wind than we thought."

"Why didn't anyone warn us?" She asked.

He grinned. "The otters never come on deck except to be let into the sea. And the dogs? Imagine a dog climbing."

She laughed to think of it and realized he was right. None of the other animals had ever done what they had just accomplished. But the rats would surely have been blown off if they hadn't realized there were two distinct sides to the mast. At least, in terms of the wind. The side that faced the extended sail was the lea side, the safest as the other side took the brunt of the breeze blowing into the sail. They were also glad for the many ropes that tied the sail to the mast and gave a good hold to the rats as they clambered up. Had they been able to watch the sailors when they went up, they would quickly have seen them take advantage of the same two things.

"Now what?" Li asked.

"We wait." And so they huddled together for warmth and awaited the dawn.

Shen-si went down into the bowels of the hold, down to where his beloved otters lived. He had been a fisherman in his village, with a small boat to maintain and nets to be constantly retied and repaired. Then he had met an old man at sea who had been using a couple of otters to chase fish into his net. Intrigued, Shen-si had begged the old fisherman to teach him how to train otters for himself. In exchange for a month's catch, the old man had agreed.

With his new knowledge, Shen-si, after working a month to pay the old fisherman, had used the otters he had found, befriended and trained, to make himself the most successful fisherman in his village. Soon he had other fishermen working for him. His fame spread, and one day a messenger appeared, from the Emperor himself, commanding his presence at the royal court. Trembling with fear he had gone. The Emperor had recruited him, and others doing the same as he, to train otters for the Great Fleet that would soon sail the world.

The fisherman had worked and trained, taken care of and fished with the otters for years now. The orders he gave them were with hand signals, but he had listened to them bark at each other and knew they had a language of their own. Over the years, he had begun to think he might be understanding them. He knew they understood him when he spoke.

Very carefully he tiptoed past the giant sloth, who seemed to be sleeping. The great creature frightened him with her mighty claws and height that towered over any man on board. She had never attacked anyone; indeed, she seemed very slow and lazy. Still, Shen-si did not believe in taking chances with a creature so large. He ducked into the opening where the otters lived, smelling the combination of animal fur and ripe fish as he did so.

"My pets," he called softly, "it is Shen-si, your master."

Two beady eyes peered at him through the gloom of the hold. It was Yong. He alerted the others. "Master Shen-si is here," he called. "Perhaps we will be taken outside."

He was right. The catch they had made just the week before had been a great one, but their ship was the fishing ship for this part of the fleet. It had been shared, to be dried for later or cooked immediately, with all the other ships. But the captains had sighted a school of tuna, and their mouths had watered. A signal using flags had gone out, and Shen-si had been notified.

"Tuna are very large," he had cautioned. "They may not be afraid of my little hunters, and thus not let themselves be chased."

His own Captain had shrugged. "It is what the Admiral has ordered. We have turned ship to intercept them. You will take your otters out in the morning."

There had been no room for disagreeing in his tone. It was a command, to be obeyed without question. Shen-si, his heart saddened with worry for his charges, nonetheless went to get them. The otters were eager to be outdoors, he could see. On deck they scrambled around, wrestling, sniffing the breeze, alertly peering over the ship's sides at the water below. As he had done many times with them, Shen-si watched and listened. The young lead otter, the one he called bright eyes, seemed especially eager. The others kept coming to him, barking at him. One bark seemed to be his name, Shen-si realized. He practiced it to himself, then spoke to "bright eyes".

"Yong?"

Yong's head snapped over to stare at the human. Had he just heard his own name from a human? "Yes, master Shen-si?" He barked back.

The fisherman's eyes widened in amazement. He had understood that. "You know my name?"

"Of course, master," Yong laughed, "we hear your men talk to you all the time. We know your speech, but now, you know ours?"

Shen-si, made speechless by astonishment, could only nod.

"Then tell me what we hunt today."

The other otters had gathered, barely moving as they watched Yong and Shen-si in conversation. Shen-si used the human tongue, but seemed to understand as Yong barked in otter back at him. The otters' play, their never-ending movement had stopped, overtaken by curiosity.

Shen-si watched them gathered around, and he knew they were all listening to him. Their curious faces and glistening eyes, their sharp-toothed mouths now seemed to smile at him, meeting his gaze in a friendly, but now unnerving, way.

"The Admiral has ordered that we catch tuna from a school the fleet spotted."

"Tuna?" Yong asked.

"They are big fish with a yellow fin who swim in mighty schools with powerful force."

Yong listened, spoke to those around him, who barked answers so quickly Shen-si had trouble following. Still, he picked up words now and then. "Yes, we know them." "They are big and trouble." "It is a challenge, let's do it."

Yong turned back to him, a fire in his eyes. "We call those yellowfins. They are mighty and do not fear us. But we can turn them."

Just then the Captain approached. He had watched Shen-si as he did so, wondering at the way it seemed the man was actually having a conversation with the otters. Then he decided it was like himself and Pek. He often felt he could almost understand his little dog, so he would make up the words he thought his pet might have said. We are all a bit foolish with our animals, he chuckled to himself.

"We have been signaled by a ship up ahead," he told Shen-si. "We are approaching the school of tuna. Have your otters ready. I will tell you when."

He walked back to his Captain's station.

"Did you understand that?" He asked Yong.

"Of course. We will be ready."

The otters all scrambled to the opening in the side railing, the board that slid open when needed. Shen-si watched for the Captain's signal, all the time amazed at what had just happened in his life. His two helpers would arrive soon, their watch beginning just when the sun came over the horizon. The skies were still a little gray, although the entire eastern sea glowed with yellow as the sun was about to appear. He would ask them if they, too, understood the otters. He did not think so. But he would ask.

Ling had heard the otters bark, had seen them scamper around the deck, then had watched as they had gathered around Shen-si. Li slept on, exhausted by their night's journey up the mast. Down below everything seemed small and insignificant.

"I thought the otters would not be out today?" Li surprised him by appearing at his side.

"You're awake. No, they did not think they would. Usually a catch such as they made last week, so they told me, would mean they would not be needed for some time. Look, there is why." He pointed to the west where the waves splashed in golden reflections of the sun that had just appeared on the eastern horizon, peeking its sleepy head like a golden god awakening.

Li looked, seeing only waves at first, but then..."They're so big!" Large fish jumping out of the water, in a giant school that seemed to extend across the water ahead of them. Another junk's sails could be seen far off that way.

Ling frowned. "Much bigger than our otter friends," he said. "I wonder if that is a problem?"

Bao was wondering the same thing as the otters slid into the sea on Shen-si's command. The fisherman had seemed worried,

The Otters of Ruapuke

and Huang had thrown Bao a concerned glance, but Xun and Yong had simply laughed.

"Yellowfin will be a new adventure," he had said when she'd asked. "We'll hunt as a group and not separate, so we have someone by us if they get frisky."

Mei had rolled her eyes. "We three girls will hunt with you tough men at the back of the school. It looks so large, it will take all of us."

"Fine with me," Yong yelled, setting a fast pace as they swam for the school.

On board the ship's men were yelling orders as they began to unfold the giant net that would soon be dropped into the sea. They had boats to lower and gaffes and pikes to handle for bringing the fish on board. No one seemed to notice the fishing master worriedly talking to his two assistants.

Li meanwhile had been scanning the skies for the little petrel they were supposed to find. She saw a bird, flying high overhead, and pointed it out to Ling. "It doesn't look so little."

He noticed that, too. The bird was floating in place, using the air currents and its wide-spread wings to hover and scan the ocean for food. The ship, still moving, came closer and closer to it. "That's not our bird," Ling decided. "Much too big for what Yong described." He began to search the skies for another bird. He watched the otters for a moment, swimming strongly in the great ocean waves, moving smoothly together towards the school of large fish. He admired how they swam, so effortlessly through the water.

Then he saw it. A smaller bird, skimming along the water as if walking on it. Amazed, he watched and wondered. "Look, Li," he said, "I think that's our bird."

"Where?" She asked.

He started to point, when a shadow fell over them. He looked up in time to see a large beak snapping at his neck. Just in time he ducked, and the bird missed. Li screamed as it snapped at her. It was the bird they had seen on high, a Grand Petrel, a larger cousin of Stormy's, which loved to eat nothing so much as small creatures it could catch. The rats had come into its sight as the ship sailed into view and it had quickly flown down to snatch a meal. Now it hovered in the wind right at the mast snapping its deadly beak at the two rats, hoping for a meal.

Had it been a hawk, or an eagle, the two rats would be dead. Viselike talons would have gripped them and taken them high away to be eaten. But this bird had webbed feet, and so must rely on its beak to snatch a meal. Ling and Li cowered in the nest, trying to avoid the sharp beak that snapped at them again and again. Soon it might find a way to land inside the nest, and then their doom would be sealed.

"We must climb out and clamber down the mast," Ling panted, dodging again and again. "Follow me when I distract it."

He had decided on a desperate measure. He would wait until the bird came straight for him and spit in its eye. If he missed, he would be dead. But if he hit, he hoped the bird would be startled enough to let them get away. He watched his chance. When he stopped moving, the petrel immediately came at him. This time it managed to land in the nest. It was now or never.

Ling watched the bird begin to aim a deadly grab with its razor sharp beak. Instead of dodging as before, he filled his mouth and let fly a stream of spit at the large, unblinking eye before him. Splat! It hit dead on, and the bird screeched in surprise. Ling and Li jumped for the top of the nest...

Just then a mighty wind slammed into the two rats, tearing their claws from the mast and sending them hurtling towards the sea below and death in churning waters!

Chapter 12 How Pek came to hear the story

Stormy had hung around the giant ship for many days, enjoying the garbage thrown overboard periodically, and hoping to catch the otters again to talk. He had liked them, they seemed to know about having fun. When he had seen them dive overboard he at first had wanted to come talk to them. But he saw quickly they were all business, swimming mightily towards a school of yellowfin he saw in the distance. He decided to wait until they finished their work.

He spent the time skimming over the waves with his wings outspread and feet dancing on the water. The Grand Petrel overhead had not gone unnoticed. Little petrels like Stormy stayed out of the way of the Grands. They were crotchety and no fun, and would fly at him and try to hurt him for no reason. He hoped the Grand would grow bored and go away.

But he'd watched in dismay as the large bird had done just the opposite. Something high in the mast of the ship had gained its attention. Stormy looked on, curious as the Grand seemed to be trying to catch something high overhead. Then two small objects appeared to fall from high in the mast towards the sea, directly where Stormy was looking on.

When they first had fallen, Ling had shouted to Li, "Spread yourself out. Let the air hit you as much as possible. It will break your fall. I hope." He knew that small animals like himself could often survive high falls.

Then he had been so busy following his own advice he hadn't had time to watch Li. The winds buffeted him as he spread out arms and legs wide. He continued to fall, of course, but slower, slow enough, he hoped, to survive the fall into the water. Of course, if the fall did not kill him, he knew the ocean would. He feared he would either be a meal for a sea creature, or would he drown trying to stay afloat. But there remained the faint hope that if he and Li could stay alive until the otters returned, their friends just might be able to save them.

"Splash!"

"Splash!"

Ling hit the water. Moments later so did Li. They both came up for air, choking and paddling furiously with their legs to keep their heads above the rolling waves.

"We're alive!" Li exclaimed joyfully. Ling wished he felt as cheerful.

"Yes," he said, "now to stay that way."

But then he saw something far off that dismayed him. It was a sharp fin coming out of the waves. What had Yong said about such a fin when telling his story of the last catch? He remembered. "Li, we must work our way to the other side of the boat. That," he pointed, "is the fin of the white killer Yong told about. We're in danger."

"The boat is leaving us," Li answered, "we're in danger anyway."

He saw it was true. The ship had continued to travel, its sails still full, making a path towards the school of fish and the hunting otters. The little rats began to swim frantically, but it was no use. They could not possibly keep up with the ship.

"Too fast, too fast," a voice from nowhere was heard.

Then they both saw him. A small bird walking on the water towards them. In an instant Ling knew who it must be.

"Are you Stormy?" He asked.

"I am, I am. But you can't stay, can't stay. You must get back to your ship, ship. Here, grab my legs, legs."

They both wondered at this. The little bird obviously wanted them to grab on to him so he could fly them to the ship. But he seemed too small and frail for such a task. Still, Ling thought and he could see Li thought it too, what choice did they have? They swam over to him, jumping up at the same time to grasp a different leg each. The little bird spread his wings and began to pump the air. Up, down, up down went his feathered muscles.

To their immense surprise, they began to rise into the air, and soon they were flying towards the mighty ship just ahead of them. They rose and rose, catching up to the moving ship as the two rats hung on, astonishment and gladness filling their hearts.

"Where shall we land, land?" Stormy asked them.

So amazed had he been to be rescued, Ling had almost forgotten why they had been there in the first place. But Li had remembered. She watched as they approached the ship. Now she spoke to Ling. "Isn't that a window to the Captain's cabin in back of the ship?"

He looked. There was an opening, and the Captain's cabin was on the top deck aft of the ship. "It must be," he answered.

"Stormy," she said, "do you see that small ledge back of the ship where the opening is?"

He peered ahead. The little bird didn't know much about ships, so it was good she had said opening and not porthole. And back instead of aft for that matter. He saw what she meant and nodded. "I see it, see it. Shall I land there?"

"Yes!" The two rats exclaimed together.

Stormy set them down as carefully as if he'd been doing it all his life. He landed with them, eager to talk to someone, and if it couldn't be the otters, these two would do. Also, he was very proud of having rescued them, for he had seen right away how awkward they were in the water. Not at all like the otters.

"All right now, now?" He inquired.

Li caught her breath. So much had happened so quickly. Part of her remained amazed they were alive at all. The moment they had begun to fall she had expected to die. But they hadn't, thanks to Ling's quick thinking and advice, and the sudden arrival of Stormy. She smiled gratefully at the bird.

"Thank you, thank you, Stormy," she gushed, unconsciously repeating herself as the petrel did. "We would have died without you."

"Not creatures, not creatures of the sea?" He asked her, although he knew the answer.

"No. We are rats, and though we seem to be on every boat in the world, we are really land animals. We don't swim well," Ling answered the question for her. He now realized why they were at this porthole. He had been peering in, and he spotted Pek. The little dog had spied shadows moving by the window and had his head up, curious. He nudged Li and pointed. She saw the little dog approaching.

"Friend Stormy," she said, "our otter friend Yong told us about meeting you and what you said about the new young Emperor. Is this true?"

"Yes, yes," Stormy bobbed his feathered head up and down rapidly. "The young Emperor said take apart all ships, ships. Kill all animals. Dogs, otters, must mean rats too, too."

Ling saw Pek peering at them, a puzzled look on his face.

"You can't mean all the animals," Ling told Stormy, "after all, some are favored pets of humans, like our Captain."

Stormy hadn't noticed Pek. He was enjoying having juicy news to share and new creatures to share it with. Petrels spend long hours at sea, day after day, without coming upon another creature to talk to and share with. Except for an occasional whale, and they never seemed interested in news of the shore. They would ask about weather and ocean currents, and when this news had been relayed to them, would disappear beneath the waves. They weren't rude, really, it's just that whales have a different view of life.

"No, no," Stormy puffed himself up and strutted as he talked, "mockingbird say all animals. Pets same as others, others."

It was more than Pek could stand. Suddenly he thrust his face out the porthole, glaring and barking at Stormy. "What are you talking about? What young Emperor, and what orders? Who are you anyway?"

Li had shrunk back against the ship's side at the dog's appearance, and Stormy had hopped off the ledge. He balanced in the air with his wings, ready to fly away. Ling stepped in quickly.

"You must be Pek, the honorable Captain's beloved pet," he said smoothly. "We were just discussing with our new friend Stormy here the news he brought from China. The old Emperor that sent this fleet out has died, and his son has become Emperor. You remember the young prince who sent you to the kennels, don't you?"

It was a story everyone had heard, even the rats. Pek's face clouded at the memory. "Stupid young twerp! You say he's Emperor now? You mean Sharpe's story was true?" He asked Stormy.

The bird was delighted to have someone new to share information with. He completely forgot his fear of the little dog and landed back on the ledge. "Yes, yes, new Emperor, young, young son of old Emperor. Gave new orders, orders, right away about the fleet, fleet."

Pek's face clouded with suspicion. "Rumors. Only rumors you know. An Emperor would only give orders from the Forbidden City. How could you possibly have heard them?"

Pek's question didn't bother Stormy at all. It gave him a chance to tell more story. "Mockingbird, mockingbird," he wagged his tail as he bobbed up and down, pacing around the ledge. Ling and Li had to keep dodging around him and several times they almost fell. Still, they didn't want to interrupt him. Pek was listening and that had been, after all, why they'd been sent on deck. "Young Emperor has a pet, pet bird who heard all. From window he shared, shared the news with the garden birds, birds. Birds talk to all, all. Finally seagull share with albatross, albatross share with Stormy, Stormy. All animals to die, all ships to be taken apart, apart."

Pek growled, gnawed for a moment on his own back leg with a tooth to ease a scratch, then shook his head. "Doesn't make sense. We're the greatest fleet the world has ever seen.

Why would the Emperor of China want to destroy this? It will bring glory to China."

Stormy cocked his head and stared with one eye, the other kept a lookout to the sea, hoping the otters would return. He had no idea how to answer Pek. The answer wasn't in the information he had, and he had no idea how humans thought or why they did anything. Since he had nothing more to share, he suddenly decided to leave and find Yong.

He flung himself into the air and began beating his wings. As he flew away he called back, "Go to find otters, otters. Good to meet, meet you."

They watched him fly away. Li with a sense of dread. She had hoped Stormy would continue to answer Pek's questions. They had to have the little dog on their side, she knew, and at the moment he only seemed annoyed, not convinced.

But Ling had been thinking about Pek's question. Unlike Stormy, he knew quite a bit about humans. Ling had lived for a time in a warehouse in Shanghai. There he had watched the humans and their strange passions. The owner of the warehouse had had a son, a spoiled son much like the young Emperor. He, too, had been jealous of his father.

"The glory would not be his," Ling said to Pek.

"What? What's that you say?"

"These ships," Ling continued, "when they return, you're right, they'll bring glory to China with their tales of vast adventures and incredible travels. But the glory will be for the old Emperor, not the young. Everyone will be talking about his father, ignoring him. He can't have that. He's got to be the one everyone pays attention to. And the only way for that to happen is to destroy all of this," Ling waved an arm to indicate the ship, then ended by pointing at Pek, "and anything that might remind people of it."

When he stopped, Pek stared at him. The little dog seemed to be thinking it over, his face wore wrinkles all across his brow. He yipped suddenly, just once, then motioned to Li and Ling. "Come in. We need to talk."

Li hesitated. Pek was a dog after all, and they were rats. Dogs killed rats. Ling, too, felt fear. But what could they do? They could not remain on the ledge. They could not scramble up the sheer side of the ship, and remaining here meant death by starvation, or another predator like the Grand Petrel. Inside was their only hope, even if it meant going completely against rat logic to trust a rat catcher dog like Pek.

Chapter 13 The return of the white killer

Mei flew backwards as the tuna shoved against her. She'd been trying to nip it in the tailfin to make it move in another direction, but the large fish had reacted by aggressively charging at her. She'd dodged enough not to be bitten, but had been forcibly shoved by the fish anyway.

"These fish aren't scared of us, Bao!" She called to her friend.

"I know," an exasperated Bao replied, working hard not to be chewed on by one of the tuna she had charged at. "Someone needs to tell Yong this isn't working."

Huang, who had had no success either, volunteered. "I'll swim back and see if he has any better ideas."

The school swam in a slow circle, feeding. The large tuna either ignored the attempts of the otters to make them move in the direction of the ship's nets, or if annoyed, individual fish would attack. They had been trying for some time now with no success. Huang found Yong and Xun on the other side of the school, frantically trying to nip at the tunas' tails and having no more success than the female otters had.

"This isn't working, Yong," Huang told him. She turned on her back to give her weary limbs a rest. "They're just too large to be afraid of us. You need to tell Shen-si to bring us back on board."

Xun waited for Yong to make a decision. He respected his friend, but he agreed for once with Huang. Nothing they had done had turned the tuna or seemed to affect the school in the slightest. He paddled in place, waiting for Yong.

The young otter watched the other two as they waited for his decision. He knew they were right, this school was not going to move for them. Still, Yong was stubborn and hated to admit defeat. But it was true, the fish were big enough that the otters only annoyed them, never frightened. It would take something a lot larger...

And then in the distance he saw it, the giant dorsal fin.

"Huang, Xun," he commanded, "the two of you get the others and swim very hard for the ship." He saw their giant ship, rolling in the waves with its sails half struck, the fishermen in small boats below it tending the nets whose ends floated on circles of cork while the bulk of the nets remained under the water, waiting to catch up the fish when they came. "Hurry and go!" he yelled.

Xun and Huang frowned and eyed each other. Yong had that dangerous tone in his voice. "What are you planning?" Xun asked.

"Something I can't even think of doing as long as the four of you aren't safe," he snapped back. "Now, please, get the others and swim as hard as you can for the ship." Huang decided there was no point in arguing. Besides, she would be glad to be done with this frustrating hunt. She flipped to her front and swam strongly around the school and back to Bao and Mei. Xun hung back, worried.

"Whatever it is," he said to Yong, "I can help."

"You are my brave and true friend," Yong told him, "but this is something that one can do, but two would be a problem."

Xun puzzled over that, and while he did, he saw what Yong had seen, the white fin in the distance. Suddenly, he knew what his friend planned. "Yong, that's crazy. He'll catch you and eat you this time."

"I hope not. But if I have to worry about even one of you he just might. Once I get him to this school he'll forget about me and I can rush to join you at the ship."

"But how will that help catch the tuna?"

Yong pointed. "If I lead him in just the right direction, he'll arrive at the school and panic it into racing away, right for the nets."

"You'll have to keep changing directions to stay away from those jaws of his," Xun pointed out. "It will make it nearly impossible to be going the right way when you reach the school." Yong frowned. "I know, but it's the only thing I can think of doing."

"On the other hand," Xun smiled, "if there are two of us, we can trade off having him chase us and make sure he's going the right way when we hit the school of tuna."

There was truth in what Xun said, but Yong hated to think of his friend being caught by the white killer. He wasn't altogether sure he himself wouldn't be. Which was, of course, what made Xun's suggestion a good one. Two might be able to keep the killer distracted enough that they could both live to lead it to the school of fish. The whole plan had frightened Yong when he'd thought of it, but the safety of his friends had been so much on his mind he hadn't dared ask any of them to help him. Now that Xun had volunteered, he found himself relieved.

"Okay. But let's be extra careful in planning this."

They both looked to make sure that the female otters had headed for the ship. He saw that Bao was behind the others, and she had turned in the water to raise her head and stare at them. He wished he could reassure her, but he certainly knew sharing his plan with her would only make her stay. "Go on," he waved, "we're fine."

She was too far away to read his face, but he knew she would be frowning and wanting to come get him. He continued to wave her on until she finally turned herself around and began to swim after Mei and Huang. Waiting until the two had reached the small boats around the nets, he shouted to Xun, "Okay, my crazy friend, let's see if this works."

The two made sure of where the white fin was moving leisurely through the water and swam, heads up and alert, towards it. The closer they approached the more the fur on the back of Yong's neck stiffened. His heart raced and he felt almost dizzy. This was madness, he began to think, why didn't I just go back to the ship and admit defeat? But he knew why. The otters had made a name for themselves among the humans with their skill and daring in the water, the way they skillfully hunted the schools of fish time after time. The pride of his people was at stake.

He glanced at Xun. His friend's fur also stood upright at the neck and his eyes were wide with anxiety. Yong had almost decided to call it off when Xun yelled, "This is the craziest thing we have ever done, Yong. But what a story we will have to tell if we live!" Then he laughed with a loud yipping cry.

That did it. Yong couldn't have turned back now for anything. The two otters raced after the killer. When they came upon him, though, they wished they hadn't.

They were still a distance away when the killer rose out of the water and turned its head to stare at the two otters with cold, steel-gray eyes. A light gleamed in them and the intelligence behind those gleaming orbs was a terror to behold. It snapped its jaws like a metal trap, the sound crashing to them across the water with a frightening intensity. Then with a speed that made the hair all across their bodies stand up, the killer submerged and came at them, jaws wide and eyes gleaming.

"Let's go!" Yong yelled.

He and Xun split off in opposite directions, but not too far apart, swimming strongly and waiting to feel the displaced water behind him that meant the killer was about to strike. Yong knew Xun would do what they had both planned depending on who the killer chased first. They had talked it over hurriedly, now he hoped their plan worked. But when Yong felt the sudden rush of water behind him he almost didn't react, so surprised was he. He had been concentrating too much on what he needed to do that it had almost numbed him to the real thing. But he recovered quickly, leaping up out of the water and arching back as the white leaped right behind him. The creature was impossibly agile and fast for something so big and deadly. Its jaws snapped closed just inches from his back paws.

Yong swam all the way under the creature as it turned, ending up going the same direction he had been at first, while the killer had to turn its great body around once more. He knew the next time it would anticipate this and he would need to go in another direction. Sure enough, when he felt the rush of water and leaped, the white had leaped back, waiting for him to reverse. But this time he went hard to the right and once again the jaws snapped in futile rage missing him. But the giant killer immediately flung itself in his direction and Yong felt the weariness in his muscles. He could not keep dodging without a rest, and this creature did not seem to need rest.

It was then, when he felt he could not strain his muscles one bit more, that Xun flashed across the killer's nose, diving and swimming hard back towards the school of fish. The white seemed to roar in rage and began to chase Xun. Yong pulled up in the water, turned on his back and gasped for air. He realized then how crazy his plan had been. Had Xun not stayed to help him, Yong knew, the white would have eaten him. He watched his friend dodge and leap away from the killer. Impossibly close to Xun the jaws snapped in anger as he again missed his prey.

Suddenly the great killer had crashed into the school of tuna. Startled, the fish found a frenzied hunter with gaping jaws gulping them whole into its mouth and ripping them apart, taking his anger at the otters out on the fish. The school, which had been placidly swimming in a circle, now exploded into panic, swimming frantically to get away. Yong had joined an exhausted Xun and they watched in pleasure as the tuna raced right for the waiting nets of the ship.

"Whew!" Xun breathed. "He almost had me."

"Me, too. Thanks."

"You'd have been lunch if you'd tried this alone," Xun laughed.

"I know that now."

"That's what friends are for, Yong. I have your back."

They watched the killer chasing the school, eating and terrorizing them. A thought occurred to both of them. "I hope he gets full," Yong said.

"Yeah, because he's between us and the ship."

They began to make their way in a wide circle away from the white killer towards the ship.

Bao, meanwhile, waited on deck where Shen-si had brought the females aboard. "Where are Yong and, Xun is the other male?" The fisherman asked. He had begun to learn their real names.

"They're crazy," Bao cried, for she had realized what Yong planned the minute she arrived on deck and saw in the distant sea the white killer's fin. "They're trying to use the white killer to scare the tuna to the nets."

"That is crazy," Shen-si agreed, fear in his voice, and yet something else. Admiration, Bao realized. He admires us. She had an inkling, then, of why Yong was doing what he did.

They watched as the otters led the killer to the school. When Yong leapt out of the water and the great jaws almost got him, Bao screeched in fear. Then she was joined by Mei and Huang, who trembled at her side as Xun, too, faced near death. Then the killer reached the school of fish and they all watched amazed as the frenzied school raced away, right for the waiting nets of the ship. Then they saw the two male otters begin to make a circled approach to the ship, away from the school and the killer.

"We need to get the basket lowered for them," Shen-si said.

But Bao was watching something else. "Do the white killers ever get done hunting?" She asked.

"It certainly ate enough of the fish to be full," Huang snorted.

But Mei saw what Bao saw. "Then why has it turned from the school and back towards Yong and Xun?" She asked.

They all saw it. The white had turned around and was headed where the two otters had last been. What it would do when it discovered them not there was anyone's guess, but Bao feared it had not finished hunting.

"Is there another small boat we can lower?" She asked the fisherman.

He immediately saw what she meant. He shouted to his helpers and they rushed to untie a boat from where it was kept, turned over and lashed down, on the deck. The otters went to help. Between them, they had the knots undone in record time. The two helpers had stared at first as the otters helped and their master seemed to be talking to them, and listening to their answers, but Shen-si had yelled at the two men to work and they soon accepted the craziness as part of this whole voyage across impossible waters and lands that had consumed two years of their lives.

In moments the boat was lowered into the water, the three otters and master Shen-si aboard, the two helpers ready on deck to lower ropes if needed. Shen-si showed the otters how to use the oars. In no time they were pulling mightily for their friends. And none too soon, Bao saw, as the white had realized his prey had moved and began to swim in hunting circles to pick up their scent. When it did, it would be swimming for them with all the skill and deadly abilities it possessed. They pulled hard on the oars and yelled to Xun and Yong.

The two otters heard them, about halfway between the shark and them, and began swimming hard to their small boat. It was then the white killer rose mightily out of the water, eyes gleaming, sighted them all and began to swim with a speed and ferocity that churned the seas around it into white foam.

Chapter 14 Meeka does not mean meek

When Snitch arrived in Bruno's lair, he found his boss in a rare good mood. The ugly rat fairly beamed with pleasure over something he had done. Snitch knew he would find out in a moment, he just worried what danger it would put him in.

Bruno came and forcibly pushed Snitch into a corner of the room, then went and peered through the opening to see if the rat had been followed. He came back and pushed the other rat down, then knelt beside him. "Listen," he whispered, "what do you know about a bag of rice that was spilled in the sloth's hold?"

"A bag of rice..." Snitch almost shouted in amazement. Bruno quickly put a hand to his mouth.

"Shh. No one must know."

"But," Snitch's voice could barely be heard now, "a bag? Unheard of. The humans have been hoarding the rice fanatically, with the dogs on guard around it."

Bruno shrugged. "Nonetheless, I have heard it is so. I want you to take a handful of our rats and go get as much as you can."

Snitch's eyes grew wide. The standoff between the Italian rats and the Indian ones had made stealing food nearly impossible. One group or the other always followed any rumor of food, and the fights over any found drew a vigilant Pug, causing them to scatter before they could bring enough back to satisfy either side. Most of the rats were starving, and getting desperate. Something like a bag of rice would make them crazy.

"I'll be followed," he whined, "and Saraj's men will kill us and take it themselves."

"Nonsense. Take five of our most clever. You know all the secret ways. You can do it." He stopped and fixed Snitch with a cold glare, "and you will do it or I'll slice your throat myself."

Snitch found himself staring at a sharp blade aimed at his throat. He gulped. "O...Okay, Bruno. I'll get five rats and go now."

"Good. And don't come back without the rice."

Nodding and still staring at the knife, Snitch backed out the door. He disappeared. In a moment, another rat entered the room. He motioned to the door. "That was Snitch going for the rice?"

"Yes. You spread the rumor that he was, didn't you?"

The other rat smiled. "Sure did. Saraj'll have half his men going after it. Snitch is one dead rat." He paused and eyed Bruno. "We all thought he was your favorite."

"Don't have favorites," Bruno growled. "Only tools. And he was no longer useful. Watch things," he ordered, "I'm off to see a dog about a rat problem in the lower holds." He gave a sinister chuckle and departed.

Pek peered out the porthole, then took a step onto the ledge. He motioned for Ling to join him. Hesitating only a moment, Ling did so. Pek had listened carefully to the whole story, hadn't menaced the two rats once, had even offered them a welcome bite of food. Still, Ling wasn't sure he was convinced, or if he did believe them whether he would help. He carefully moved onto the ledge, eyeing the little dog.

"What is it?" He asked.

Pek motioned with his head out to the water. "Something's going on out there."

"The otters were sent to hunt some fish. Big ones it looked like," Ling told him.

Pek sniffed the air. "I smell danger, and fear."

Ling leaned out and let his nose gather in the smells. Salty air, men and boats, the faint hint of otter...and blood! Suddenly he smelled it, and then the fear that Pek had mentioned came in a rush to his nose. The ledge ran all along the stern of the ship. It had probably provided a foothold for the workmen who had built the ship. Ling couldn't imagine it being used on the sea voyage. It was too narrow and unsteady with any kind of rolling sea for the humans. But a rat...Ling ran along the ledge to where it ended and peered around to the ship's side where he could see the fish being hauled into the giant nets not too far from the ship.

He wondered about the smells. The catch was coming in, everything seemed just fine. Then he saw it, off farther out. A giant white killer shark, like the one, or even the same one that had nearly eaten the otters on their last hunt! It was speeding in the water towards two small bobbing heads swimming hard for a frail looking boat manned by three otters and a human.

"What do you see? What do you see?" An impatient Pek called to him. He looked back to see the dog had put one paw up on the ledge, and Li's small face peering at him beside the little dog.

He explained quickly, then looked back in time to see a small brown form leaping in the air with a giant white killer, open mouth bristling with razor sharp teeth, coming out of the water after it.

Yong and Xun had made it almost to the small boat containing Shen-si and the female otters when they felt the powerful force of water moving behind them. They split as before, but Yong felt the white's pursuit of him and leaped out of the water, the massive, deadly jaws snapping at the air behind him. He came down into water and leaped immediately once more, a good thing because the killer chomped at the water right where he'd been. It roared in mindless rage at the miss.

Yong saw Xun being hauled aboard the small boat and raced for it. The boat had turned and was paddling frantically away, but he knew he could catch up, and so did they. He did so leaping out of the water for the boat as he felt the driving force of water behind him. Yong landed practically in Bao's lap, turning in time to see the white killer flying over the boat, eyes smoldering with hate and jaws snapping as it passed.

They all screamed, even Shen-si.

"Row, row!" Yelled Huang.

Then something smashed into the side of the boat, nearly capsizing it and causing it to spin crazily. The shark had rammed them. They saw it swimming in a tight circle, ready to come around again and finish the job. It was then they heard the cannon roar. They looked at the ship where the bronze cannon that fired signals to the other ships had been pointed at them. A large harpoon had been placed inside it and it landed not far from the ship, hissing into the water, then surfacing as its wooden shaft caused it to float to the surface. Shen-si reached over the side of the boat and grabbed it.

He held it, hands shaking, as the white killer approached. "Everyone grab it with me or he will be too strong for us!"

The otters all placed their weight behind it as they prepared for the impact of harpoon and shark. Bao closed her eyes, holding on with all her might.

"Now!" Shen-si yelled.

The collision flung all of them back, almost flipping them over into the water. They felt the harpoon torn from their grasp as their mighty attacker pulled away in pain and shock. They could see the shaft sticking up crazily into the air as the killer zigzagged in the water, trying to shake off this hated weapon that had pierced its side.

They gratefully saw it swim away, slamming the water time and again trying in vain to free itself from the harpoon. Then it submerged and they lost sight of it altogether. The human and otters collapsed into the boat, exhausted beyond belief, but relieved just to be alive.

A short time later they were hauled aboard the great ship where they found that the harpoon had been the Captain's idea. "You saved our lives," Shen-si bowed to him.

"I could not lose my mighty hunters," he beamed, proud his plan had worked, "especially after bringing us the Admiral's tuna."

For Snitch, everything about this had smelled wrong. He never had trusted Bruno, but now something in the rat leader's manner had seemed particularly wrong. If he could have seen Bruno at that moment, alerting Pug and suggesting the rat killer bring Chow and Bok along to the hold, he would have known just how wrong it was. As it was, making his way with five large and fierce rats he had chosen, he started at every unknown sound, every strange smell.

The hold as they approached seemed empty except for the large sloth who lived there, Meeka, Snitch seemed to recall being her name. He motioned as they left the protection of the dark shaft they had come down for his followers to stay right behind him. Sniffing, he tried to locate the rice, but the smells in this part of the hold overwhelmed anything else. There was the sloth, her large pile of aromatic leaves, the hole that led to the otters... and dog! He clearly smelled dog. Sharpe for sure, and the one called Shih. He stopped, totally panicked now.

"Come on, Snitch," one of the rats with him whispered, "let's find the rice and get out of here. I smell dog, as well as stuff I never smelled before. Giving me the shakes."

"Me, too," another of the rats said. "I just want to get it and go."

"Then spread out and find the rice," Snitch snapped back, "because I don't know exactly where it is."

"Neither do we," a voice interrupted them, "and we've been down here a while. We're beginning to think something's not right."

It was Saraj and over twenty of his followers. Snitch and his five froze. "Hello, Saraj," Snitch tried to make his voice as pleasant as possible, "didn't expect to meet you here."

"But I'm betting Bruno did. I'm thinking," Saraj snarled, "that he meant for us to find you here and kill you. I thought this rumor sounded too good."

"Then why'd you come?" One of Snitch's men demanded.

"Too good to pass up if true. Now it looks like killing is the only thing for us here."

"Listen, Saraj..." Snitch began, but he never finished.

Three dogs hurtled into the hold, jaws snapping at rats and eyes gleaming for the kill. Chow, Bok and Pug had their choice of targets, and Snitch had been Pug's first. He was about to snap the rat's neck when a large force picked him off the ground and said, "Let him go."

His mouth opened more in surprise than obedience, dropping Snitch, and he was flung into a large pile of leaves where he lay stunned for a moment. In quick order, a large paw grabbed both Chow and Bok and held them, dangling helplessly while snapping and growling, into the air.

"No killing in my hold," a voice spoke.

The rats, with a chance to flee, found themselves stopped by the sight. It was Meeka, who had been roused from dreams of home by the uproar, and had moved remarkably quickly for a sloth when she saw what was occurring. The two big dogs were helpless to resist her incredible strength and after a moment quieted and waited, unable to escape, in her grasp. Even Pug, slowly recovering, decided to wait where he was.

It was then that Sharpe and the otters showed up. The big dog had come with them after their harrowing experience with the white killer. He had watched it all from the ship's deck and came down now to the hold with them, his big heart concerned but also happy about their rescue. They burst upon the scene of chaos in the hold.

Sharpe immediately ran to his friend Meeka. "Are you all right?" He asked.

The rats, when the otters and another dog had entered had faded into the crevices and holes that led to safety, but still they remained to hear, curiosity eating at them. Meeka quickly explained what little she knew. "I awoke to find these dogs trying to kill these rats in my hold. I don't know why they are here."

Yong could smell the rats still waiting and called out, "Friend rats. What has brought you down to our friend Meeka's hold?"

Saraj cautiously stepped out to meet with Yong. He stayed close enough to dart back to safety if he needed to. "There were rumors of a bag of rice down here," he said, "but I see now that it was a trap by our friend Bruno to have us killed. He even tricked his own worthless Snitch into coming."

Meeka slowly set Chow and Bok down. "If I let go, will you refrain from killing?" She asked.

Bok

Chow nodded, and after a moment, so did Bok. She let them go. They moved immediately away from her and worked at straightening the mangled fur around their necks. Pug walked out from the leaves then and waited by himself. The rats all stayed clear of him.

"You foolish animals," Meeka chided them, "the humans will kill you all when you return to China, and you spend this time helping them?"

Pug's head rose sharply. "What does she mean?"

The otters and Sharpe began talking at once. Then Hui appeared in the doorway of the otters' hold. "Be quiet," she ordered in her calm tone. She could barely be heard, yet they all stopped.

"Tell them of the petrel," she said to Yong.

Yong eyed the crowd around him, the rat-catching dogs with eyes narrowed still in anger, the suspicious rats, his own good otters and Meeka who had surprised them all. He quietly told them of Stormy and the story of the death of their beloved Emperor to be replaced by his son, the untrustworthy one. When he explained what the mockingbird had heard about the ships to be dismantled and the animals put to death, there were mixed reactions.

Chow growled, "Lies. We are royal dogs, Bok and I. No Emperor would have us killed."

The rats argued among themselves. "Humans always try to kill us." "If we make land, we can get off the ships alive." "Still, we need to work together or we might not live to make land." "Truth."

Sharpe listened, sitting near his friend, Meeka, taking it all in. The wrinkled brown dog never changed expression, but Bao had begun to know, and like him, and she could see he was planning something.

Hui saw it, too. The elder otter had also come to like and trust Sharpe. He was the one dog the otters felt they could depend on. She whispered to her band of otters, Mei, Bao, Yong and Xun, except for Huang who had left to see about Zan and Pipi, "Be ready to back Sharpe. Whatever he says, we are behind him."

They nodded. All of them felt the same about their wrinkle-skinned friend.

"Pug," Sharpe said quietly, but not so quiet that the others couldn't hear if they listened. "What would make you stop hunting and killing the rats?"

The rats immediately grew silent, listening.

"What do you mean?" Pug was suspicious, but also wary. The news of the old Emperor's death had shaken him.

"If we all work together," Sharpe told him, "we might possibly live. But only if we work together."

Digesting this, they saw the little dog think. Slowly he nodded. "If it is as you say, that foolish young Emperor in charge, then perhaps he would have us killed upon our return. He is no lover of dogs, this I could see when he came to the shipyard. In that case, if the rats worked with us, I would stop." He said.

"Don't be a fool!" Chow snapped at him. "We dogs are in no danger. It's all lies."

Pug's scornful glance spoke volumes. "Oh, and you know this from the contempt we were shown that day the young prince visited and had Pek moved to the kennels?"

"Only fair," Bok commented, "no favorites. I liked him for doing that."

"No pets," Sharpe reminded him. "And a man who does not see a dog as a pet, does not see us as valuable. It's an easy step from there to casual murder of dogs."

He could see that the two big dogs were shaken by this, but they also were stubborn. Chow growled at Bok, "Come on. We don't need to hear this nonsense. If you won't kill rats," he snapped at Pug, "don't expect mercy from us. You will be useless, like the Captain's worthless pet." And they left.

Saraj, with the two large dogs gone and Pug's words still in his head, approached the otters. "Is there a plan? If there is, count my rats in. We might survive when we reach land, but till then it would be nice not to be dying." His glance at Pug had meaning.

"We have one," Hui nodded at him, "but it all depends on the little pet, Pek. Have we heard from the two, Ling and Li? Our otters did not sight Stormy."

Huang had given her a brief version of the day's adventure, it was this that had brought her up to see the other otters, and run her into the confusion in the hold. It all still depended on convincing the little dog, and no one knew if any convincing had taken place. Sharpe shook his head as she glanced at him, and the otters all shook theirs.

"If you need Pek," Saraj said, "then it must mean you plan to do something with the ship itself, correct?"

Yong answered him. "Yes, friend Saraj is it?" The rat nodded. "We mean to wreck it into the first good land we come to. But it is so large, and we have no idea how to even start to do such a thing. But Pek does. Sharpe says he gives orders as if he were the Captain himself. So we were hoping to find the little bird to convince him."

"You have already spoken to him?"

"I did," Sharpe said, "but he was not convinced. I'm not sure if even the little bird will, but it seemed our only chance."

Everyone grew quiet a moment thinking of it. So much depending on one little, foolish pet of a dog. It was a sobering thought to them all.

"Friend Sharpe," Hui spoke finally, "will you go see if you can find our two rat friends?"

But Sharpe only snuffed, putting his head between his paws for a moment. His soulful eyes were sad and teary when he glanced at them again. "I do not think it is well with our two friends," he told them. "They climbed to the top mast last night, but in the light of day I watched for them to spot the bird, but the wrong one came. A giant petrel I think and it attacked them."

"What!" Gasped Bao. She had come to like the two rats.

"It grabbed at them and they fell to the sea. It was the last I saw of them," Sharpe ended sadly.

Before more could be said, a voice spoke. "And the last we thought we would see of you, our friends. And yet it proved to be the greatest luck of all, falling into the sea."

Out of a knot in the wall emerged Ling and Li, and their friends rushed to greet them.

Chapter 15 Hard-won friends

Shen-si struggled with his feelings that evening as he lay in his bunk below decks. There were over fifty men in the crowded area where he slept. The Captain had a cabin, as did the visiting dignitaries from Vietnam, India, Burma, Cambodia and Sri Lanka. They had with them wives and consorts, but the regular sailors and crewmen like Shen-si shared a large sleeping area with bunks that gave them just enough room to stretch out in. He could hear his two helpers, Chen and Dong, snoring already in their bunks, exhausted from the day's excitement.

But for Shen-si, his entire world had changed. Before, he had been enchanted with his charges, the otters, as skilled and intelligent animals who relied on him as their master to give them orders and take charge of their huntings. But today… they were like another race of people, he realized. They had a language and felt for each other as friends and family just as he would his own people. It had opened his eyes to them in a way that caused him to lie sleepless now.

Among their talk he had heard hints of some deadly danger to them. At first he had thought they meant the white killer shark. But slowly it had dawned on him that that wasn't it at all. Now he worried and wondered if he should go below, to their hold, and find out more.

All of which should also have amazed him. I can talk to my otters, he thought. What a wondrous thing. For these many years I have worked with them, and I have heard them speaking to each other, but, he realized with a start, I never really listened to them. I heard sounds, the sounds that all animals make, I thought. But when I finally listened, really listened as one does to another person who speaks, I heard words. He wondered if it was the same with all animals. The very idea frightened him, as well as excited his soul. The gentle motion of the ship as it churned through the ocean waves usually lulled him to sleep by now. But these thoughts, whirling through him like a tornado, would not let him rest.

With a sigh, he rose from his bunk, slipped his feet into his sandals and made his way quietly from the room. He encountered many crewman as he went, on a new shift, or just being relieved from one, but they paid him no attention. Such a large ship had men constantly moving about as they went to their jobs, or to eat, or to sleep. Still, part of him waited to be stopped and asked his business. It was a part that dreaded, and then secretly hoped, to share his news. But Shen-si was a sensible man. He knew that no one would believe him. Even Chen and Dong, who had been right there with him as he conversed with the otters, had not believed him when he tried to explain it to them.

Not long ago, I would not have believed them either, he told himself.

As he approached the hold where the giant sloth lived, the one that led to the otters' den, he heard voices. Startled, he did not enter right away but waited at the entrance to the hold, listening.

"We are not sure what Pek will do," a voice was saying. "He is almost convinced that the petrel carried truthful news, but he still does not want to believe that his Captain could not save him. Li and I have done all the talking he will hear from us about it."

"Sharpe," a voice Shen-si recognized, the otter Yong, spoke, "you know him better than any of us. Can you convince him?"

A barking came, a dog it seemed, and at first Shen-si did not understand it. But then he told himself to listen, and, "...tried, but Pek is a stubborn one. Perhaps we need to give him time."

Shen-si almost missed the next speaker, so amazed was he that he had understood a dog. "Even with his help," a small, squeaky voice spoke, "I'm not sure how we animals could wreck this gigantic ship upon a shore. I know we must try, but it seems beyond us."

Overwhelmed by curiosity, Shen-si peered into the room. The voice speaking at first seemed invisible. Then he located it, and nearly fainted from shock. It was a rat! He stumbled into the room, crying out, "Are there any animals that do not talk?"

The rats squealed and seemed to disappear, the otters raised their faces and regarded him with their bright button eyes. A large creature, the sloth he realized, rose from the pile of leaves, chewing slowly and eyeing him with a mixture of interest and fear. The dog, Sharpe he recognized at once, merely raised its head and then after a moment's glance, turned to the otters. He did not see Pug, who sat by the pile of leaves and so was hidden by Meeka's bulk.

"Is he a friend of yours?" The dog clearly asked.

"Shen-si, our hunting master," Yong explained. "Master, what are you doing here?"

For the first time, Shen-si felt the danger of his position. He was not merely a human come upon some animals, he was a human who understood their speech, and had heard them talk of wrecking the ship. The hair rose at the back of his neck and his skin trembled.

"Forgive me," he said, "all of you. I could not sleep and so...I have only recently learned to listen to you, oh, wise animals, and now I know things a man, perhaps, should not know..." He stopped, without a clue how to continue.

The gentle female otter, Bao he remembered, came to him and touched him gently on the forearm. "You are the first human in a long time to listen, friend Shen-si. Long ago our legends tell us, the master Lao-Tsu also learned to listen, and so became a sage and gave much wisdom to the humans. Perhaps you, too, can do this. For now, if you will help us, you may stay. But if not, I fear you must go before you hear more."

Lao-Tsu! He who had compiled the book of wisdom for the Chinese? He had learned it from the animals? Shen-si was stunned. Like all good Chinese, he used the words of Kung-Fu-Tsu to be wise around family and friends, and Lao-Tsu to understand the ways of the larger world. He had merely thought of this as wisdom Lao-Tsu had gained from meditation. That it had come from the animals...made perfect sense he realized.

He sat, Lotus fashion, and spread his hands to them. "How may your humble servant help?"

Then from the walls appeared the rats, moving cautiously towards him. He did not dare move himself. "Can he be trusted?" A large rat asked.

"Yes, Saraj," Bao answered, "I believe he can. For a human, he is kind and decent."

"Well, if he is, he's the first I've known." But the rat stayed in the middle of the room and the talk began again, this time with the animals looking to Shen-si to see what the human would say and do.

"Pek did mention," another rat, Ling, Shen-si would learn, said, "that if we approached a shore and there was a storm, it would be easier to founder the ship on the rocks.

"Can't very well make a storm come, can we?" Another rat opined.

"Is that our only chance, a storm?"

"Slim chance then."

Others spoke in the same way, and gloom settled on the room.

But Hui, who Shen-si knew as the wise matriarch of the otters, spoke up. "Shame on all of you. The Creator Spirit who made all life, even humans," she nodded at Shen-si, "can do anything. If that Spirit wants us to be saved, then there will be storm and we should be ready for it. Did Pek say what to do if there was a storm?" Ling smiled at Hui. "He did, most noble otter. He said that two things would be most important; keeping the sails from being struck, and controlling the rudder. He did not say how to do these, but perhaps our friend Shen-si can suggest?"

The fisherman blushed. He had sailed ships in his day, small junks that hugged the coastline and brought in the catch from small nets. Never anything close to the colossal ship they sailed upon now. Still, there were certain truths about all ships, and that is what Pek, the Captain's dog he realized, must have meant.

"There are ropes used to bring down the sails," he said, "and they are tied off around the deck so that crewmen can easily untie them and pull them in. If someone were to cut those ropes so that they moved freely, especially in a storm, they would be very hard to regain control of in a storm." The animals nodded. Their teeth could gnaw, so when he spoke of cutting they immediately thought of ways to do that.

"And the rudder?" Yong asked. "What is that?"

Of course, they would not know about the rudder, he realized. He tried to explain it to them, how it moved the ship's direction and kept them from floundering at sea. The otters remembered seeing it and began to describe it to the others. Shen-si knew that it might be beyond the ability of the animals to do anything with it. As huge as the ships were, so were the rudders. The one on this ship, he knew, was as tall as 7 men standing on each other's shoulders. It took several crewmen working together to control it.

Shen-si told them as much. He saw them frown, but no one seemed dismayed. In small groups they discussed the problem, trying to find a solution. The fisherman did not know what amazed him more, that they had such skills of language, or that they could reason so like men. He only knew that in the last hour or so, his whole view of life had changed.

He knew now from them that there was a new Emperor, and that he had ordered the fleet destroyed, and the animals on it. Perhaps he would be permitted to return to his village and take up his trade again, but somehow, he could not imagine doing that any more without his beloved otters. And to allow them to be killed...he shook his head. He could not let that happen. But to stop it, to throw in his lot with the animals, was to say goodbye to his beloved homeland forever.

As he watched the animated Yong, the sweet-faced Bao, the eager little rats and the earnest dog, Sharpe, he knew what his decision must be. There was right, and there was wrong. A man had to choose between them, and then live his life with that choice. He knew that he could never be able to convince the others onboard ship, and that throwing in his lot with the animals would make him a traitor to the humans, but he had no choice. He must do what was right.

A peace descended upon him, a peace that would be shattered moments later by the little dog he had not noticed until now. Pug had been sniffing the air, and he came from behind Meeka, who had remained silent, having said all she had to say earlier, and gave a yip that gained all of their attentions. The rats seemed ready to dash away, Shen-si noticed, nor could he blame them for he recognized the little dog immediately as the rat killer on board the ship. But the dog's words surprised him.

"I don't smell Snitch," Pug said.

The rats immediately searched for him. Two of those who had come with him, came sheepishly forward. "We stayed, because we have decided to join you. But Snitch and the others we came with, after they heard what you planned, left. We think they went to tell Bruno."

"You know what that means, don't you?" Pug demanded.

Yong shook his head. "We live down in this hold, friend Pug, and we don't know the ways of the rest of the ship."

Pug gave a small nod, then turned to Saraj. "But this one knows, I bet. Snitch is Bruno's puppet."

"You think he would return to him now?" Saraj spoke with amazement in his voice. "Bruno tricked Snitch. He set a trap to have my rats or the dogs kill him."

Shaking his head, Pug gestured with a paw at Saraj. "Clearly you don't know how Snitch thinks. But I do. He has been alerting me to rat movements for two years now. First with the Chinese rats, and lately with your Indian ones. He cannot function on his own. He needs someone to take orders from. I'm sure you would not want to use him, would you?"

Saraj shook his head. "Never. We have lately come to know the truth of what you say about him. We would never trust him."

"And so he must know, he has no place with us," Hui spoke up. "I see what you say, little Pug. He has returned to Bruno with information he hopes will help him regain his place. And Bruno will know that he cannot depend on being boss of the rats while there are so many who hate him. So he will join with Chow and Bok."

The thought stunned them all. Rats had never worked with dogs, not in the memory of those here. And yet impossibly, they had to admit, Bruno and Snitch had been doing so for two years. And the dogs had worked with them.

"Why would Chow work with rats?" Saraj asked.

"Because he thinks to go home to China," Sharpe spoke, "and he thinks everything will be just fine with the new Emperor when he does. He thinks the only chance of stopping us will be to throw in with Bruno."

"But the facts..." began Saraj.

Sharpe laughed. "You do not know Chow. Or Bok. Facts mean nothing. He believes what he believes." The kindly dog's face became very grave. The others listened somberly as he continued, "From this moment on, all of us are in danger. Chow, Bok and, yes, Bruno will stop at nothing to make us fail, including doing everything they can to kill us if that is what it takes!"

Chapter 16 A decision to return

Snitch's heart pounded as he approached the rat lair. He knew without a doubt that Bruno had set him up, knew he'd been meant to die there in the hold with Saraj and his rats. Three dogs. He shook his head, wondering at the narrow escape the rats had known. Alone, he had come back, slowly and suspiciously in case Bruno had another trap in mind for any rat who made it back alive. Saraj, he knew, had thrown in his lot with the otters and their allies. He would try and help them wreck the ship. What a fool!

The size of the great ship, the teaming number of humans who manned her were known to them all. Snitch could easily see how hopeless the thought of taking control of it was. Yet there they were, even now, trying to think of ways to do so. He shook his head. To stay with them was death. He just hoped that returning to Bruno wasn't the same.

"What choice do I have?" He groaned aloud. Then peered around the last corner of the tunnel before entering the lair.

A hand came from around that corner wrapping itself around his throat and pulling him in. Before he could react the other arm of his attacker had grabbed him and he found himself being throttled by the enormous muscles of a large rat he recognized as Pietro, one of Bruno's ready stooges. And then, as the breath was forced from him and his eyes began to glaze over with a red haze, he saw Bruno's leering face.

"Not quite yet, Pietro," Bruno ordered. The pressure on his windpipe relaxed, although the grip on him didn't.

"Bruno," he gasped in a wheezing breath, "you must listen..."

"So you got away," Bruno sneered. "Should have known you would. Probably left the others to die and scurried back, didn't you? Well, it's too bad, but we can take care of that."

"No," he tried to speak but it came out in a weak whisper, "you've got it wrong..." he gasped, unable to continue for a moment. He worked hard to swallow and get his lungs working again.

"What did I get wrong?" Bruno demanded. "Three dogs against a score of rats? You seem to be the only one making his way back here." He turned and pointed. Snitch saw a dozen of Bruno's henchmen waiting behind him with clubs. "We've been waiting to finish off any who managed to survive. So far you've been the only one. And now I'm tired of talking to you." He motioned to Pietro who began to tighten his paws on Snitch's windpipe again.

"They're all still alive," Snitch managed to gasp out before his air was cut off and the red again began creeping into his vision.

"What did you say?" Bruno had turned to leave and now he whirled and stared at Snitch. He knew the little rat might be lying to try and save his hide...still, it had been odd that he was the only one to make it back. He made a gesture to Pietro and the rat again loosened his grip on Snitch's throat. He waited impatiently while his former helper gasped for air and tried to swallow. Finally he couldn't wait and he reached out a paw and gripped the fur around Snitch's chest, pulling him close and staring with narrow, bloodshot eyes into the other's face.

"What did you mean, "they're all still alive?" Where were the dogs?"

Snitch, eyes wide with fear, answered, "The giant sloth grabbed them and stopped them. Then the otters came in and they made the dogs leave. No rats died."

His brow furrowed and his eyes narrowed to slits. "The giant sloth? She has nothing to do with rats. Why would she do that?"

Snitch shrugged. "I don't know, she just did. So I hurried back to tell you that they've all joined together, Saraj and his rats, the otters and that sloth, to plan to how to wreck the ship."

Bruno snorted laughter. "Fat chance of that."

"That's what I thought, so I hurried to tell you." Snitch had left before Shen-si had arrived, or he might have altered his opinion.

"Always know which side of the rice has the sauce, eh Snitch?" Bruno chuckled. He made a move to Pietro to release Snitch. The big rat did. He also motioned to his waiting men to leave. "Go back to your females and litters," he ordered. "I'll call you soon and we'll plan what to do." They left, but Snitch noticed that Pietro didn't. So, he thought, he's the new one by Bruno. He shrugged. It didn't matter to Snitch as long as Bruno let him live.

"Come with me," he ordered Snitch. "I need to think this through."

Bok paced back and forth on deck as the wind screamed through his fur. They were sailing in a minor storm, and while normally the dogs would have scrambled below to find a safe, dry spot to escape it, Chow had insisted they come on deck. He was agitated, biting at anything that got in his way. All the human crew had quickly realized this and were staying far from the two dogs. Bok felt it, too, and he paced trying to make sense of what had happened in the hold earlier.

"Who was that large animal down there?" He growled. Unlike every other animal, Bok had no curiosity about the expedition's findings. Until this time he hadn't given Meeka's existence a moments thought.

"It's a sloth," Chow snarled.

The big dog stopped pacing a moment. He had seen sloths in China, they were small and slow, living in trees where he couldn't get to them.

"Too big for a sloth," he answered.

"Not a Chinese sloth," Chow told him, "she's from one of the lands we came to."

Bok shook his head. "It was big and powerful. More powerful than I would have thought. Nothing has ever picked me up like that before. But it took us by surprise. If we could surprise it, I think we could kill it."

Chow thought about it. If the Captain found them in the hold killing one of the expedition's prizes, they would be in danger. Still, if he had a chance he'd love to rip its throat out. It had embarrassed him, and Chow wouldn't forget that. Not since that day with the Emperor in his forest...he shook his head, snuffing and scratched the deck with his paws. But he doubted they could sneak up on it, not with the rats around, and the otters. One or the other of them would smell he and Bok before they could get to the sloth.

"We can't be the ones," he told the other dog, "though I'd like to. Too many friends of hers down there, so we probably couldn't get close enough without her being warned. We have to think of another way."

"You need Bruno," a voice said softly.

Both dogs' snouts snapped towards the sound. It was Snitch, they recognized his voice, but they couldn't see him. Wisely, the little rat kept out of reach. He spoke through a crack in the deck, below them and unreachable. He could see them but they couldn't see him. They could hear and smell him, though.

"That was a bad trick of yours and Bruno's, telling us to go to the hold and get the rats," Chow accused.

"Yeah, but the trick was on me, not you," Snitch told them. "You were supposed to kill all the rats, including me. Only, Bruno didn't know about the sloth."

"But you're working for him again," Chow said. It wasn't a question.

"The coward's got nowhere else to go," Bok yipped. He could feel the rat squirm and he smiled.

"Bruno agrees the sloth should die," Snitch said, ignoring their comments.

"Good, then he can do it."

Snitch sighed. "That's what he's planning right now. And then in exchange for doing that, he wants the two of you to kill Saraj and his rats."

"And after that he'll have us kill you, no doubt?" Bok asked. It hit home. Snitch was afraid of that very thing. The dog knew it. Bok had a streak of cruelty that made him smell Snitch's fear, and enjoy it.

Snitch sighed. "You'd kill me any time you had the chance, wouldn't you?"

"With pleasure," Bok answered.

"You're a rat, Snitch, what did you expect from us? Now, let's talk about the sloth. How's he plan on doing it?" Chow asked.

Snitch sighed. He knew that Chow spoke the truth. Dogs killed rats. Still, he wished...he guessed he'd just have to be careful. "I don't know. He just said to tell you to be ready when he says it's safe to go back down there."

Chow didn't like it, but then, he'd never liked working with a rat to catch other rats. He snuffed again, then said, "Tell him we'll be waiting to hear from him."

He heard the rat's feet padding away. Bok looked at him quizzically. "How much longer are we going to take orders from a rat?"

"After the sloth is dead, we'll catch Snitch and make him lead us to Bruno," Chow said.

"How? We're too big to get at most of the places the rats hide."

Chow nodded. "But Pug isn't, and I know he's more tired of Bruno's orders than we are."

Bok snarled. "Pug! He's changed sides, the little traitor."

"No," Chow said. "They just confused him with that talk about the young Emperor. He'll realize it's crazy and come back. And even if he doesn't, he'll want to kill Bruno. He's a rat catcher, it's what he does."

The wind picked up and then rain began pouring down on them. They ran for the lower deck and dryness.

Chapter 17 What Pek and Shih heard

Shih marveled at Pek's sleeping pad, just as he was meant to. It had been very unusual of the little dog to invite Shih into the cabin, and Shih knew how important Pek was to the group. He had come up on deck, which he seldom did, just to see if he could gain Pek's confidence. The little dog had been happily in his place, the warm sun shining down on him, yipping at the crew telling them to work harder. The crew had great affection for their Captain's little pet, and they smiled at him often as they worked, and nodded as he encouraged them.

"You are indeed important to the ship," Shih had commented.

Pek had greeted him, but only casually and he had been waiting for an opportunity to compliment the small dog. Shih knew how vain Pek was. Indeed, the compliment had done its job. Immediately after he'd said it, Pek had lifted his head and smiled. "It is true," he had replied. "My Captain depends on me to soothe him after a hard day of work, and my crew need me to urge them on to do their best. I have kept this ship sailing safely for some time now."

Knowing better, Shih did not smile at this outrageous claim. In fact, being a Buddhist, he did not know that it was not true. After all, what good karma might Pek have brought aboard, or what bad thoughts the Captain or his crew might have had without the little pet being aboard? So Shih remained placid-faced at the remark, merely nodding in agreement.

"Would you like to see my cabin?" Pek asked on a sudden impulse. He always thought of it as his own, though it belonged, of course, to the Captain.

"It would be an honor," Shih answered.

Thus it was when the Captain went to his cabin that afternoon, calling for Pek to follow, Shih tagged along. The Captain noticed, but being a Buddhist himself, appreciated the wise little dog that trailed after his own. He saw it as a good omen. Inside, he brought out charts and began to study them as Pek showed off his fine sleeping pad and dinner bowl. The two dogs were engaged in looking at Pek's many chew toys when the first mate arrived.

"You wanted to see me, my Captain?" He inquired.

"Yes, please come in." The Captain motioned at the table where he had spread out the chart. "This is a copy of the mapping that has been done of the island we have been sailing around for weeks now. It seems," he pointed to the map, "that it is really two islands, a northern and a southern one. The southern one is full of high mountains and forest. It is also much colder. But this northern one has on the west side a small inlet the Admiral would like us to visit. It is a somewhat forbidding harbor for our large ship, but we can anchor outside of it and take long boats in to the shore. Natives have been sighted and we are to try and meet with them, to tell them of the Emperor of China and give them gifts from his magnificent generosity."

The mate had bowed when the Emperor had been mentioned, now he straightened up. "And you wish me to lead the landing party?" He asked. It had been thus before, and the Captain was pleased his first mate was so trained to remember and know this.

"Yes. We will set the four anchors just outside the harbor, if the waters are so shallow to allow it, and wait for you."

The mate pondered it. He had had some experience in the past with natives as they had sailed the world, not always good. "What does the Admiral say about these people? Are they friendly? What weapons do they possess?"

The Captain nodded. "Those are very good questions. The Admiral has written me that they have observed the people hunting in large boats for whale. They are very adept with the harpoon, but only for hunting. When our boats have approached they have not threatened us or seemed inclined to do harm. Indeed, he says they seem friendly and have gestured for us to meet with them. Some meetings have taken place on other parts of the islands, and all has gone well. So I think we need not fear."

The mate sighed in relief. He knew their voyage neared its end and he heartily wished to live to see his beloved China again. He began to calculate which long boats and which crewmen to take on the shore adventure.

Meanwhile, though they had paid scant attention at first, the two dogs had found themselves listening avidly when the mention of anchoring the ship had been made. Shih watched Pek, for to him much of it was not clearly understood. The Captain's pet had frowned, and continued to do so as the conversation progressed. Finally, Shih asked him, "What so concerns you, my friend?"

Pek had forgotten for a moment that Shih was there. He started, then cocked his head and pondered it all. He did not know where Shih stood with what first Sharpe, then the bird and finally the two rats had told him. But he did know this was information they would dearly love. He began to think what to say when the human, the mate, spoke again.

"How far are we from this harbor?"

"Two days sail southeast. Barring a storm, we will be there then. Can you be ready in that time?"

"Yes, my Captain. Shall I go begin?"

The Captain, pleased at his mate, smiled and nodded. "It is the Admiral's wish, and mine. Let me know how things go and if you need me for anything."

The mate bowed low. "It will be as you say." He departed.

"You heard?" Pek asked Shih.

"I did. What does it mean?" He could guess, but he needed to hear from the Captain's dog, for he knew much depended on him.

Pek, when he answered, was surprisingly blunt. "Where do you stand on the plans to wreck my ship?"

"My ship." Shih had heard the words clearly, and he knew to tread lightly here. Anything he said Pek would take personally. Perhaps, though, information could be gathered here.

"I know," he smiled and stood calmly and without passion, "that there is some desperation among them. I try never to feel such emotions."

This made Pek wonder. It was true, Shih never did seem to have emotions, not like the rest of them. Chow and Bok, they were ruthless, and they knew anger and how to channel it. Pug usually seemed fairly cool about what he did, but there was a deep pride, Pek knew, in the little dog and his skills as a hunter. Sharpe...he shook his head thinking of his friend. Kindness was the dog's main attribute, shining from him like a light. And Sharpe had believed the bird.

"What do you think?" Pek asked. "Could the bird have been right? Could our Emperor be dead and the young upstart in his place?"

Shih weighed what to say. He knew much depended now on his words. It was clear that Pek remembered the Young Emperor as the young Prince who had treated him badly. Perhaps he needed to see things as they were more clearly.

"Did you chance to catch sight of our Old Emperor come to see us off when the fleet sailed?" Shih asked.

"Of course. His soldiers, his courtiers, a great crowd of the nobles and their ladies, all to see the great fleet leave," Pek answered proudly.

"But did you see the Emperor himself?"

Pek thought hard. He had seen the magnificent litter, carried by twelve servants in royal silk garb, with pendants held aloft and a fine silk parasol over the litter in purple and gold. But the Emperor had stayed in the litter, only waving with a hand as the fleet set out.

"I saw him wave."

Shih sighed. "Life is a lamp-flame before a wind. Though his burned brightly and well all the days of his life, I fear it had begun to flicker at the end, even as we saw, too weak to do more than watch from his litter. He was a magnificent man, a great Emperor, perhaps one of the greatest. But his son," Shih made a motion with one paw that indicated something small and unworthy, "did not appreciate him. Perhaps, if the flame truly did die, the son fears it might be brought to life again by the greatness of what this fleet has done. The father, than, might eclipse the son even in death.

"Of course, only a small and less noble heart would think such a thing. Not an Emperor who deserved to be so. Maybe I misjudged him from that visit he made to our shipyard, when you were…" he paused and pretended to search for the word, all the time watching Pek's face, "encouraged to join the rest of the dogs in the kennels."

Pek's face had grown grimmer as he listened. Scowling now, he ground his teeth. "There is nothing noble in that one."

"But surely," Shih asked innocently, "even he would not do what the bird claims, have the fleet destroyed and all the animals, even the noble dogs, destroyed too?"

"You think not?" Pek barked. "You did not see his meanness when he took me from my master and made me stay with the rest of you." He was unaware how his words might sound, and Shih took no offense, knowing the little dog as he did. "He might indeed order such a thing."

Shih waited patiently for Pek as the other grew quiet. Think it through, he encouraged with his thoughts, remember and ponder the young prince and what he was like. For he is indeed Emperor now, Shih felt this as a certainty, though how he could not have said. In the dim shadows of the cabin, as the sun set and the flaming rays danced on the ocean horizon far to the right of the ship, he waited for Pek to make up his mind.

Ling regarded Saraj with a touch of humor. The leader of rats from India had treated Ling with something like contempt for months, simply on the basis of Bruno's lies. But since that day in Meeka's hold, he had been trying in every way to be friendly, to the point of almost ignoring his own rats to be with Ling. Still, Ling knew what was behind it. A part of Saraj did indeed want to be friends, but the other part knew that of any of the rats in the hold, Ling would know Bruno's weaknesses, and strengths, best. Saraj feared Bruno and what he might do, and he desperately needed to know exactly what that was.

Li had noticed it, too. She had smiled sadly as they talked of it. "He is the leader of his group of rats, Ling, with no place to lead them. Bruno has him trapped down here because of the dogs and the other Italian rats. So he is desperate. Be kind to him, we need his friendship."

So Ling listened now as Saraj talked.

"We need to know what Bruno plans," Saraj said for the umpteenth time. "He's clever, and cruel. There's no telling what he might do."

"I agree. But he's watching all the exits from the hold closely. Between his own men and the dogs, we're trapped."

"My men are trapped, it's true. And the five rats who used to work with Bruno are so demoralized they don't want to do anything. But, Ling, you are not like them, or like my rats for that matter. Our wives and families are still in the rats' lair. Bruno won't hurt them, at least, I don't think so, because he needs their numbers. If he wants to build up again to escape the ship went it reaches China again, as he believes it will, he needs them. Besides, he knows we won't do anything desperate to him as long as he holds them hostage."

A note had been sent to that effect from Bruno. The Indian rats had cried with dismay upon reading it, for Bruno made it clear in the note that if they tried to come at him, to attack, he would kill their families. Saraj seemed to think it was a bluff, but Ling knew he couldn't take a chance on it not being so.

"What do you mean I'm not like them, or you?" Ling asked.

Saraj's face grew grave. "We all have family to lose in Bruno's hands. You don't. Li is here with you. And," his eyes pleaded with Ling, "you know how to get about in this ship like none of us. You're a legend, Ling, for the way you have snuck around Pug for two years, stealing food and gaining knowledge. You alone can sneak out of here without Bruno knowing it and find out what's going on."

"I don't know of any ways out of here that Bruno doesn't," Ling said.

Saraj shrugged. "Maybe not, but I think you've already thought of ways to get out of here if you had to."

Ling was surprised. In truth, he had thought of a couple but he didn't know how Saraj knew of them. The easiest way was to do what he and Li had done to get on deck, ride in the folds of Sharpe's skin. He was sure that Bruno's rats would never expect that. And Saraj knew nothing of it, having not been part of the conspiracy then. When he and Li had returned from their adventure they had been snuck into the hold by Shen-si, riding in his pockets. No one had seen them, and Ling hadn't bothered to explain. It presented another possible avenue of escape, though he could not count on when the human would again be down to the hold.

Sharpe, on the other hand, visited Meeka every day.

"Suppose I could. What if I couldn't get back with the news?"

"Friend Ling," Saraj smiled, "if you can get out, you can certainly get back, I'm sure of it."

That was true, and Ling did know it. He grimaced. "I must talk to Li first."

"By all means. But please, decide soon. I'm afraid of Bruno and his plans. The sooner we are ready for him the better I believe."

Li, when he told her of the conversation with Saraj, didn't seem surprised. "I wondered how long before they came to you."

"Why?"

She took his face in her two paws and nuzzled him nose to nose. "Oh, my sweet and noble rat. You are too modest. When he said you were a legend, it was not merely flattery. You are, don't you know it?" He didn't.

Later in the day they found the wrinkled dog when he came to visit Meeka. Sharpe listened gravely when Ling explained what he needed. "If you could merely take me up one level..."

"Both of us," Li interrupted.

Ling started. "No, only me, Li. You must not come."

"Why? Have you not said often how softly and quietly I go about?"

"Yes, but there are other things involved in sneaking around..."

"And you think I could not do them? I might surprise you, Ling."

He sighed deeply. Then he took her two front paws in his. "Listen, my love. It is possible you can sneak as well as me. But where I go, only one can sometimes go. And if I have to be worried about you, and I will worry, no matter what you say," he interrupted her as she started to speak, "I will not be able to do my job. If I am distracted, and I would be, than I might make just one mistake, and then neither of us would return."

Li bowed her head and did not speak for moments. Then she lifted her head to reveal eyes glistening with water that threatened to flow in rivers of tears at any moment. "I fear for you to go. If something happened to you, I would not be able to go on. Please, Ling, take me with you."

But he shook his head and would not be moved though her entreaties touched him to the deepest part of his heart. "I cannot. If you wish to see me again, let me go alone. Do you not know, Li, that if I have you to return to, nothing can stop me from returning?"

Silence followed. Sharpe waited, patient and kind to the last as they worked this out. Ling waited for her to see the truth of his words. But she did not see them, instead she felt what he had said at the last, that she would be his reason for returning. She nodded then and said to Sharpe, "You watch over him." Then she kissed Ling lightly and departed to cry alone.

Then he and Sharpe discussed how they would leave together.

Chapter 18 Knowledge that
must be shared

Snitch waited where Bruno had placed him, watching the main entryway to the hold. Other rats were stationed at the usual rat exits, small holes and tunnels where Saraj's rats might try to escape. Any rat who tried would be set upon by a dozen of Bruno's henchmen armed with weapons. It would be murder, since the exits were ones that only one or at most two rats could get through at a time.

The large entryway, then, was the most likely exit. But Bok and Chow manned this station, taking turns to be there at all times. No rat who tried it would last long, even a group would be torn to pieces by the large dogs. Yet here it was that Bruno had stationed Snitch.

"That's where they'll try their tricks," he'd said. "You of all rats know about tricks," he'd chuckled to Snitch. "So I want you there to spot anything they try to do."

So far that had been nothing. Still, they only needed to watch for another couple of days. Then Bruno's plan would take care of the giant sloth, and the dogs would go into the hold to take care of the rats down there. Suddenly Snitch became alert. Bok, who was on watch at this time, rose suddenly from where he'd been lying near the exit, and Snitch rose, too. But it was only Sharpe. They had both seen him enter, Bok saying nothing to him because he hated him so. Sharpe wasn't a rat so Snitch had paid him no mind, either.

Bok lay back down when he saw who it was, and Snitch relaxed, too. He began to turn his attention back to the hold opening when something about Sharpe caught his attention. Something about his underbelly didn't seem right, like he'd gained weight in the hold...or, Snitch snapped alertly to his feet, as if something was clinging to the fur under there!

His beady eyes studied the big dog as he walked away, his gait, his balance, everything. Snitch's eyes shone. He nodded to himself, then hurried off to see someone.

Ling had breathed a sigh of relief as they made their way past Bok. He'd been afraid the killer would smell him, but he needn't have worried. Sharpe's scent was strong, and Bok's hatred even stronger. He chose to ignore Sharpe as a sign of his disdain for him. When they arrived one level up, Ling let go of Sharpe's fur and dropped to the decking.

"Thank you, friend Sharpe," he said.

"I'm going to see Pek," Sharpe told him. "I'll be on deck the rest of the day. When night approaches, though, I'll come back down. You wait here for me."

"I will."

He watched the big dog walk leisurely away, marveling again that he, a rat, could have a dog for a friend. Enough of that, he chided himself, you have only a few hours to find out what Bruno is up to. And you know he's up to something bad, so best be getting started.

There was a tunnel only Ling knew about that traveled in a torturous route until it ended just above Bruno's personal lair. It was a very tight squeeze, and if he was found out while in there it would be an easy matter for Bruno to have him killed. He'd be trapped with no escape. But he was betting Bruno wouldn't find out. Even Bruno didn't know about this tunnel. The lead rat was clever, in a diabolical way, but not smart about places to hide. He didn't need to be. He made others hide from him.

There were several dangerous moments before Ling made it to the tunnel. More than once he had to squeeze himself into an impossible angle of a wooden opening, or between a beam that protruded from a deck support. But Bruno's rats were careless, sure that their enemies were safely trapped in the lower hold. Time and again when they could have sniffed him out they seemed to not even be trying. It didn't make Ling worry any less, or keep sweat from breaking out all over him time and again. When he finally pushed and squeezed his way into the area just above Bruno's he was exhausted from worry. But he'd made it. Now he waited.

Time passed and the close space and his exertions got to him. Ling fell asleep. When he was awakened by voices, he almost gave himself away by being startled awake. Just in time he clamped his jaws around a gasp that tried to escape his mouth. Slowly he turned his head without making a sound and peered below. He saw Bruno with another rat who he didn't recognize at first. Then he did. Pietro, a large and brutal follower of the leader who apparently had risen now to second in command. Ling wondered about Snitch and his place in things. But they were speaking and he put his wondering aside.

"The rope you have found is perfect, Pietro," Bruno's oily voice smiled with pleasure. "Wherever did you find it?"

"Me and two others braved the deck. We snuck around some crewmen and chewed a piece off a big coil there. Then we waited and hurried it down here. One of the others was caught by that Bok. Killed him, Boss. I thought they was on our side?"

Bruno sighed, "Dogs are never truly on our side, my friend. When we have conquered our rat enemies, we will work on taking care of them, starting with Bok. I have found where the cook keeps his rat poison. It works well in dog food, too, I understand."

Pietro laughed. "Ain't you the one, Boss. If we didn't need them to kill Saraj and his bunch after we take care of the sloth, I'd wish you'd do it now."

"As for that," Bruno went to the opening to his compartment and peered out, "I'm afraid that the ones we send to pull the rope tight around her neck might not make it out again. So don't send anyone we can't spare."

The other rat stared at his boss for a moment, trying to take it in. "I thought we had their escape all worked out."

"We did. But that Chow has decided he wants to be in on the kill. The moment we tighten the noose he wants to come in and finish the job."

"So we'll leave then and let him."

"That would be my plan also. But he's bringing Bok, and he says he can't guarantee to control him. He'll start killing any rats he finds Chow says."

Pietro shook his head. "Don't seem right. We do the work and then he kills us. Dogs ain't got no sense of fair play."

Bruno began to laugh. He slapped his confederate on the shoulder. "Fair play! Peitro, you are a card."

Ling could see that Pietro didn't understand the humor, but he began to laugh with his boss anyway. Ling shuddered. Bruno and Chow had much in common, he decided. But when, he wondered? When would they try to kill Meeka?

"We're set for tomorrow night when the otters are asleep, Boss."

"Good. Send me the ones who will be doing it. I want to give them a pep talk. Whatever you do, don't tell anyone else about Chow and his plans."

"Okay, Boss."

He thought of wriggling out then and hurrying back to wait for Sharpe. It was obvious what Bruno planned to do. Ling knew where the rats would descend from. There was a way to Meeka's hold just above her. The problem with it was that the rats could drop down from it, but it was too steep to get back up to. They'd have to leave by the ways that Saraj and his rats would be watching. Or by the main entrance where Bok and Chow waited. He knew the lie Bruno would give to his rats, too. He'd warn them that they must leave out the hold exit, and then reassure them, falsely, that the dogs would let them go because of their deal. Reassured, they'd be sent to their deaths.

You're evil, Bruno, Ling breathed to himself. Someday someone should make you pay for it. But right now, I've got to get away. He waited until the rats sent by Pietro began arriving to squeeze himself out, knowing their noisy coming in would mask his departure. He made it down and away, then worked his way out along several tunnels and hurried to where he had decided to wait for Sharpe. It took him only a few minutes, running into no other rats this time and he breathed a sigh of relief as he carefully checked right and left before dashing across the one open space of deck he had to worry about to get to the place where he would hide the rest of the day. He didn't see anything.

He ran.

Halfway across a large canvass cloth descended from above and fell on him. He felt the heavy cloth and panicked, kicking at it desperately. Then he began to bite through it as quickly as he could. He hoped it had been dropped by some careless crewman, but he knew if it got rolled up he'd get rolled up in it. He made a hole just big enough to squeeze through and began wriggling his way out.

A paw slammed him back down, then a familiar voice spoke softly to him.

"The drop cloth was Snitch's idea. He said you'd be here, and he was right. Now I have to decide what to do with you."

It was Pug, a strange puzzled look on his face but the meaty weight of his paw canceling any plans for escape Ling might have.

Li waited for Ling's return, anxious, wringing her hands and pacing back and forth. When the kindly dog finally appeared, she rushed to him. But the look on his face sent waves of fear through her.

"Where is he?" She demanded.

"I don't know. He wasn't where we agreed to meet. I waited for him, then came to see if he had found another way back. I can see he hasn't. I'll go look for him again."

She grabbed at him, tugging at his wrinkly fur. "Take me with you."

This brought a growl, not of anger but out of the annoyance Sharpe had that something had gone wrong and he should have been aware of it. "It's too dangerous, Li. Ling's too clever to be trapped by the dogs, at least, not without the help of Snitch or Bruno. Let me find out if anyone knows anything. If they've killed him," he saw her gasp as he said it, but he'd needed that, needed the shock of it to make her see why he must go alone, "then your going won't help, and if he's still alive but trapped somehow, I can come back and we can make plans to free him."

Everything within her screamed that she must go, must find him, but her reason told her Sharpe was right. Tears flowed down her cheeks and she wrung her hands in agitation. "Then go, but come back the minute you know anything."

He nodded, and left.

Meeka had been listening. "He'll be all right, Li. You know Ling, he's so smart. He must have gotten to a situation where he couldn't get back right away to meet Sharpe. He must be waiting his chance." She said it to reassure Li, wanting to believe every word of it. But when the two, lady rat and lady sloth, raised eye to eye, they both knew that it could be so much worse.

"Thank you, Meeka," Li sighed, "it may be as you say." She hoped so, knew that the sloth had been trying from a friend's heart to calm her, and was grateful.

It was then that Shih came skidding into the room, Bok angrily snapping at his heels. Meeka moved in that deceptively quick manner of hers towards him, and Bok, with a bark of frustration, backed out of the hold. Shih, who had fallen and slid the rest of the way to them, rose calmly, dusting himself off.

"Thank you, noble sloth," he said. "It seems I am not welcome to come here anymore, at least according to Bok."

Saraj, who had watched from his hiding place, hurried to them now. "I saw him stop you at the opening and tell you not to come in," he said, "but you came anyway. What is so important, friend Shih?"

Several rat heads, the compatriots of Saraj and the five abandoned rats of Bruno's, poked heads out of holes all along the walls. Meeka was very curious, for Shih came seldom down here, and no one knew where he stood on the matter of the wrecking of the ship.

"You have our complete attention," she smiled, grabbing a cluster of leaves, inserting them in her mouth, and beginning to chew while settling back on her haunches to listen.

But he only asked, "Where are the otters?"

"In their hold," Li pointed, then asked, "Have you heard anything of Ling?"

Shih's face had returned to its usual calm demeanor. He shook his head. "No. But I believe I must speak with our otter friends." He left them in curious befuddlement and went down to the otters' den. They did not follow, not having been invited, but all except Meeka wanted to. She alone would not have fit down their hole, and had the patience to wait and hear about it later.

Shih found the otters sleeping in small groups, curled up together in units of family or friend. When he entered, though, little Pipi raised his head. He squealed, "Company, Mama," and rose immediately on his hind legs and peered at Shih.

This awakened the rest of them. In a moment he found himself surrounded by beady-eyed and questioning faces. "What brings you here at this hour, Shih?" Yong asked what they were all thinking. Wise old Hui kept silent, waiting to hear what the dog had to say. She could tell he had made a decision.

"I have been with Pek all the day," Shih began, "and we heard important plans from the Captain." He paused to scan their faces. "We will be anchoring the ship in two days beside land. It is a rugged piece of land and the ship cannot get as close into the harbor as they would like. This means the small boats will go the rest of the way to shore."

Then he stopped, and it was obvious to all that Shih had intended to say more, but now could not. The otters exchanged glances, for they knew of the sea, and of rough harbors, and of anchored ships. Those like Yong and Hui who had been most involved in fishing with humans understood what might happen, and their eyes grew bright.

"The anchor lines are very heavy, thick ropes," Hui said.

Yong nodded. "It would take two otters at each rope to gnaw through as quickly as needed. For we could not be sure to all finish at the same time, and once one goes the crew will be alerted."

"And try to stop us," Xun agreed, "so there must be two at each to finish as quickly as can be."

"Then the ship will begin to drift," Bao exclaimed, "and the waves will send it towards the shore."

"So we must find a way to disable the rudder, also," Huang pointed out.

They stopped and looked at Shih.

He smiled.

"I promised Pek I would not tell you how such a thing could be done. When he heard of the plans to anchor so, he mused aloud the very thing you just said, how the ship might be set adrift. Then he realized what he had said, and sternly gave me an order. He told me the words had slipped out, that he had not intended me to hear, and that I must not share how to do what you have just, on your own I might add, planned to do. I have not shared it, have I?"

Yong laughed and the others joined in, chasing each other and frisking merrily. Finally they stopped and returned to where Shih waited patiently. "Friend Shih," Yong chuckled, "you may safely tell Pek that no word of exactly how to wreck the ship came from your lips. But now," he stopped laughing and became as serious as an otter can get, "we need you to go to Master Shen-si and ask him to come down to us. Can you do this?"

Shih started, then shook his head. "Ask him? How would I do that? Bark at him and then he will just know? He is a human."

Bao smiled. "But a human who understands our speech, now. It is a miracle, and not only that, he is on our side."

Shih cocked his head, taking in this strange development. "So, the echo returns to the voice," he said with one of the cryptic sayings they had learned to expect from him. "It is indeed a sign, my friends. I will go to him at once."

They began speaking as he left, planning what to do if they could convince Shen-si to take them above decks. But Zan alone had grown quiet. Without warning he yipped loudly, and all of them stopped to stare at him.

"What is it, Zan?" Asked his mate, Huang.

"There are four anchors. Two at each would be all of us."

"Of course, and all us hunters will be ready," Yong exclaimed proudly.

Zan shook his head. "You are not hearing me. Four anchors, two on each side of the ship are what the Captain uses. You have told me so yourselves, many times. That means it will take all of us, including myself who is lame, and Pipi who is only a pup. In these deadly waters with a crashing ship."

And then Huang, glancing first at her mate and then at her pup understood and moaned, then fainted.

Chapter 19 The courage of Li

Pug had grabbed Ling by the back of his neck in his teeth, not in a kill bite but in a carry bite, and then taken him to the back of the kitchen and placed him inside an overturned metal bowl too heavy for Ling to lift. All during the trip Ling had waited for a killing blow, and when one did not come, when he found himself inside the bowl, his astonishment turned to hard thinking. Pug for his part had said nothing the whole trip, nor when he placed him inside the bowl, unless you counted a quick admonition, "Make no noise if you wish to survive," and then Ling had heard his paws pad quickly away.

That he should be dead, Ling had no doubts. That he wasn't, he took first for a miracle, and then began to examine the possibilities. He had not been in the hold when Pug had heard the story from the otters of the new young Emperor and the plans to wreck the boat. They had told him that Pug had left, undecided, and Ling had shrugged that away. Pug undecided was the same as Pug against them. At least, that had been his thought then.

But now...Pug really was undecided he realized. The little dog didn't know which side to be on, so he delayed being on either. Catching Ling when Snitch had given him word that Ling was about, and Ling realized now that Snitch must have been at the hold exit watching when he left clinging to Sharpe, Pug had merely done what they would expect of him. But not killing him after he caught him...well, there'd been no one there to see.

He can't decide. He can't decide, Ling kept repeating it to himself, trying to work out what it meant. For him, of course, it meant life or death. Whichever way the dog decided would determine his fate. But, though he valued his own life, Ling knew much more was at stake here. Meeka's life, and the rats in the hold, and even the otters depended on Pug's decision. For Ling had to get back and warn Meeka, had to stop Bruno's plan. He must convince Pug to join them. But how?

Sharpe, meanwhile, had found the canvas, sniffed at it and from his nose pictured what had happened there. No scent of blood, so Ling was still alive, at least when Pug, he reasoned, following this scent now, had carried him away. His mind was so concentrated on following the scent that Sharpe found himself unprepared when Chow blocked his path.

"Where are you going, traitor?"

The wrinkled dog squinted and stared at Chow. Sharing that he was tracking Ling never entered his mind. It would mean the death of the rat. Besides, he had grown increasingly annoyed with the big dog in front of him. "Wherever I want, Chow. Now get out of my way."

Without warning Chow lunged for his throat, and Sharpe only barely twisted his head to avoid the deadly move, receiving a gashing rip with Chow's teeth that laid open flesh and caused the blood to appear on his skin. Sharpe stepped quickly back, lowering his head to make it impossible for his neck to be touched. He snarled. "That was a mistake, Chow."

The other dog began edging to the side, looking for an opening. Sharpe moved with him and the two dogs began circling one another, mouths at the ready, claws padding against the wooden flooring. "My mistake was not attacking a long time ago. I intend to kill you now and end this whole nonsense about the Emperor's son."

"What if I prove to be like the boar, Chow?" Sharpe said it evenly, but he watched the other dog flinch at the memory.

Through clenched teeth Chow muttered, "That memory, too, will disappear when you are gone."

Sharpe shook his head sadly. "You do not learn, Chow. You never did."

And then he lunged high, a feint to make Chow drop back, which he did, exposing a foreleg, which Sharpe grabbed in his powerful jaws. He stepped back quickly then, pulling up and

Chow found himself lifted up and then flipped onto his back. In moments he was pinned by the wrinkled dog, who kept him unable to get up by sheer weight, though he wriggled mightily and snarled and tried to bring his fangs to bear on the other.

"I could kill you now, Chow," Sharpe said then, "I want you to remember that. But it is not my way. You must learn, although sadly you seem to not want to, that your way is not the right way."

"You sound like that idiot Shih and his Buddhist philosophy," Chow growled back.

"Perhaps he is not such an idiot, then."

Then Sharpe brought a foreleg against Chow's neck and watched as the big dog, squirming for moments, fought for air. He waited until the dog became weak and ceased resisting, then he released him, rose and went on his way. At least, he intended to.

"Quick, get him while he is no longer fighting," a voice came that should have warned him first, but then many human hands had grabbed him before he could react. "Did anyone see why they were fighting?" Another voice asked. Then a third said, "We should keep them isolated until they calm down." A rope was slipped over his neck and he found himself being dragged away. The same thing was happening to a slowly recovering Chow, too weak to resist.

The human crew had witnessed the fight, at first just one crew member, then a whole group of them as they heard the snarling and growling. A mate had come then and instructed one of them to run get rope. He decided the dogs needed to be put in safe areas for a while until they calmed down. "We can't have fighting dogs on board the boat," he told the others.

Sharpe found himself tied to a beam in one of the crew bunk areas. He assumed the same had been done to Chow, when he'd recovered. He snuffed at the rope, wondering if he could chew it apart. He chewed at it thoughtfully, but after a time decided he didn't have the right teeth for such a chore. Then Sharpe did what he knew how to do. He curled up on the floor of the deck and waited.

Li on her part remained near Meeka, waiting and hoping for Sharpe to return. She heard the otters planning and yipping as they did down in their hold, watched as an anxious Saraj talked with his followers. She sat by Meeka for a time as the sloth chewed and chewed on her leaves, methodically working them over until they could be digested. All the time her insides churned, worried and wondering about her beloved Ling. Finally she heard Bok, restless above them, barking at someone. It should have been time for Chow to come relieve him, but he apparently had not. Then Li knew things were not right and she must do something.

She had been studying the hold for days, looking for some way out the others hadn't seen. Any other rat would have given up, trusting to those in command to find a way. But Li had been around Ling too long, and had learned from him to trust no one except yourself. If he could not find a way, it did not exist. He never waited on others. She had tried very hard to think like him. Where would my Ling try to escape? She asked herself. So she had examined every inch of the hold. Now she thought she had spotted something. She sidled over to Meeka.

"Meeka," she said softly, "is that a loose board above your head?" The giant sloth, for all the time she'd spent in her hold, had never bothered looking up there. She could not possibly get out that way, and no food grew there, so she had no interest in it. Now she did, as a favor to her new friend. Squinting carefully, from a higher position than Li, she decided it might be.

"Perhaps," she answered. "Why?"

"Because, it I climb up your back and you raise one arm up high, and then lift your legs as high as you can, I might reach it."

"Why ever would you want to do that?"

"To get out of here. I must find where Ling is. I know he is in trouble, and Sharpe has not returned. Perhaps they are both in trouble."

The last worked its magic on Meeka. Ling she might have been ready to wait longer on, but the thought of her dear friend Sharpe in trouble was too much.

"All right, let me get directly under it."

Moving her slow way over, while Li balanced back and forth between her two feet and her tail impatiently, the sloth finally came directly under the board they had noticed. Li quickly then ran up the sloth's leg, to her back then up her arm while Meeka giggled, "That tickles."

The giant sloth then stood on tip-toe and reached as high as she could with the arm where Li rested. From Meeka's fingertips Li found she could not quite reach the board that hung down slightly. But, Li thought, if I ran up Meeka's arm and leaped, I just might be able to reach it. "Hold still," she commanded the sloth.

Meeka began to think of asking why she should hold so still, but by the time the words began to form in her mouth, it was too late. Li had gone back down the arm all the way back to the sloth's toes, then run as hard as she could up and up to the end of Meeka's long digits and leapt with all her might. As she sailed into the air her only thought was, "Here I come, Ling!"

Reaching her arms high above her, Li felt the board at her fingertips as her leap ended. Before she could fall back, she grasped it with all her strength and drew herself up. The opening was just enough for a rat, like her, and she carefully crawled inside it. Her heart beat like a drum and the blood pounded in her head. She felt wonderful! She listened with ears twitched, hoping Bruno's rats were not about. She heard nothing and sighed with relief.

If she had known that this was the way Bruno intended to drop down and strangle Meeka, and that just a few hours before his rats had been peering down, making their plans complete for the next evening, she would have been both terrified and angry. But she knew nothing, only that she had to get moving and find Ling. She hurried away.

The tunnel she had found led up another level, and as her heart quieted and her fear subsided, her nose began to speak to her. She smelled rats, Bruno's rats, and that worried her. But she met no one and so came to the hold where Sharpe and Chow had fought. She had been following Sharpe's scent, but now her nose told her of the battle, and she shivered with fear. Had the killer gotten to her friend? She thought Sharpe could handle Chow, but there was blood on the deck and it smelled fresh. The rank smell of humans was everywhere, but then it always was as the decks rose higher. Sharpe's smell continued that way, she felt, so she followed.

Soon she found herself in the human sleeping quarters. She trembled with fear. All the time she had been following Sharpe's scent she had been sniffing for Pug. The little dog would no doubt kill her if he found her, and she knew she was no match for his cunning as Ling was. Still, she did the bravest thing she had ever done in her life. She continued on.

Then she saw him. Sharpe was tied in a corner, next to wooden crates and some sleeping hammocks. He lay on the floor, and as she watched she saw him rhythmically breathing. So, he was all right. Sighing with relief, she made her careful way to him. It was a slow process. Humans would come in and out of the room, she would dart into dark corners while her heart pounded in her chest, wait until they left, or settled to sleep, then continue on her way.

Finally Li made her way close enough to whisper to the dog. "Sharpe?"

One ear moved back a half inch, one eye opened slightly. "Li?"

"Are you all right?"

"Of course."

"Then why are you tied up?"

He snorted. "The humans caught Chow and I fighting after Chow attacked me. They decided to tie both of us, apart from each other, so we would cool off." He shrugged.

It made her wonder. "Do you often fight?"

"No." He shook his head. "But they always worry we will."

Li had limited knowledge of dogs and their world. Rats fought often, she knew, and the male rats more than the female. It had often made her ponder the dog population aboard, for there were only male dogs.

"Why are there no female dogs on the voyage?" She asked.

Sharpe gave a surprising laugh. "The Emperor ordered that there be only males," he paused and smiled at her, "so we would not fight."

Then Li joined him in laughing. But she sobered up quickly as she remembered her mission. The hold they were in was a dangerous place for her, and she dared not stay long. But she had to find a way to get Sharpe out. She studied the hold carefully.

After taking it in she asked, "Did you find Ling?"

Shaking his head, Sharpe sighed. "I didn't have a chance. Chow found me while I was following his trail."

Li had been studying the rope that held Sharpe, and she was sure she could bite through it in no time. She glanced left and right, there were no humans watching. "I can bite through the rope and free you."

"No," Sharpe said, "not while it is still so busy. They would simply catch me and tie me up again. We must wait for the midnight watch, when less crewmen are about. That will give us most of the rest of the night before the next watch to find Ling."

"When will that be?" She asked impatiently.

"I'm not sure. See that hammock over to my left, with the arm of the human hanging down?"

She turned to gaze in that direction, saw who he meant and nodded. "Yes."

"That man has the midnight watch. When he leaves, we can go, too." With that the wrinkled dog settled back down. Li could see it was no use arguing with him. She thought of going off on her own to find Ling, but knew it would be too dangerous. She would need the big dog to cling to in order to get to certain parts of the ship where Ling might be. With a sigh she, too, settled to wait, finding a good place in the shadows of the many wooden crates.

Li had fallen asleep when bells chiming awakened her. She saw Sharpe open his eyes and followed his gaze to where the midnight watch man lay. The man rose, rubbed his eyes sleepily and pulled on a shirt, then slipped into his sandals. He left the room along with a dozen others. She waited for a sign from Sharpe. When he nodded, she ran and began to gnaw the rope.

She had been following right behind Sharpe as he sniffed the scent of Ling for some time when she dared to ask, "How do you know he is not dead?"

Sharpe stopped. "Because I am following his scent, which obviously had been moving."

Li regarded the big dog, trying to see if his words were trying to reassure her only, or if he really believed this. "A dead rat would be carried to be disposed of, would it not, and thus be moving?"

The big dog squinted, thinking. Then he spoke, "When I first scented Ling, he had been trapped under a canvas by Pug." She gasped, but he continued quickly, "Pug carried him away, but there was no blood scent, no death. Ling was alive. Now I am following to see where he carried him."

If he had thought to reassure her, he was mistaken. Li was more worried than ever. Pug was a rat killer, all the rats knew that. If he had carried Ling away, it was only to kill him in a more convenient place, or maybe to toy with him first. "We must hurry," she begged.

"I know," he said. He turned to go again.

It was then that Pug stepped into their path. In his mouth he carried something that he had been dragging behind him. He saw them and smiled.

"So, the rescuers are come. The trail ends here," he indicated the way he had come.

And then they both smelled it. Hot peppers, crushed by Pug's feet and smeared along the way. It would foul the most sensitive nose. Li had instinctively jumped behind Sharpe when she saw the rat killer, now she emerged recklessly to confront him.

"Where is he?" She demanded, her eyes blazing with emotion.

Pug smiled. "Such bravery in a rat. I take it you are a friend of Ling's?"

She nodded, unable to speak a word more.

"Then you will be glad to know he is still alive. For now."

Chapter 20 The ship finds the harbor

Shen-si had eaten, then he had wandered to the upper deck of the ship, to watch the waves as the vessel neared land after being so long at sea. Like all of the sailors aboard, he had been appraised of the plan to anchor off a harbor while a boat went to meet with the natives. It had been done more than once on their long voyage, but now it meant more to him. Anchorage, and shore so close. How can I get my otters to safety? He paced the deck, staying out of the way of the crew working the sails and the rudder, but always worrying the problem. The fresh sea air was invigorating, and he hoped it would stimulate his mind.

He had moved to the very bow of the ship, staring as the vessel cut through the water, slicing white waves on either side, when Shih found him. The little dog watched the man for a bit staring ahead, the wind billowing his shirt behind him, causing his pigtail to fly aft. Shih worried that he would speak to the man and have him only respond as men did, patting his head and speaking nonsense in return. But the others had said he would understand, so finally Shih shrugged and spoke.

"Master Shen-si," he barked, "I have been sent to find you."

The man whirled in surprise, regarded the dog with a frown, but he didn't lean over to pat his head. Instead, he said, "I don't know you, do I? You are not the rat catcher, Pug. Who are you?"

Shih smiled. Now, those were intelligent comments. "I am Shih. I do not often come around you humans, you are often too simple for me. So, you really do understand the talk of animals?"

The other smiled ruefully. "It came of a sudden, though I feel such a fool for having worked with and listened to my otter friends for so long and never having made the effort to understand. But now I do. And," he sighed, "I, too, have found that most humans are too simple. My own men would not believe me when I tried to explain it to them."

"Most of the crew talk of gambling, fish and women," Shih asserted.

Shen-si laughed. "That is true." Then his face grew solemn. "But you said you were sent. By whom?"

"Your otter friends."

Shen-si took this in and responded immediately, "Then we must go to them at once."

They began to make their way to a stairway to go below when one of the many ship's mates stopped Shen-si. "Fisherman," he said, "the Captain wishes to see you as soon as we have made anchor. He said for you to wait for him on the foredeck by his cabin."

"When will we make anchor?"

The mate frowned at the question. Captain's orders were never questioned. So he ignored it. "Come with me," he demanded, and turning his back began leading the other to the foredeck.

Shen-si had hoped to be allowed to go below first, but he could see it was useless. He whispered to Shih, "Tell them what has happened to me, and that I will be there as soon as I can."

The mate turned. "Were you speaking to me?" There were no other crew around them, only the little Buddhist dog.

The fisherman gulped. "A bad habit of talking aloud to myself," he explained.

This made the mate frown further. "It is as the others say about you. Too long have you been in the company of those otters of yours." He began to lead Shen-si again, walking more briskly than ever so that the poor man nearly had to run to keep up. Shih had left already. Shen-si was glad. He hoped the dog hadn't seen the expression on the mate's face. Clearly the sailor thought Shen-si was a madman.

Then the poor fisherman realized he had worried that a dog's opinion of him might drop. I am a madman, he thought.

Chow had been tied for some time, pacing and growling so that no crewman dared approach him. He did not realize this made it more and more unlikely he would be untied. He only knew how frustrated he was, and how more determined than ever that Sharpe must die. But he also knew he could not do it alone. Chow was smart enough to admit that, and clever enough to see that with Bok, the two of them could kill the wrinkled dog.

Finally he wore himself out and settled in a sitting position. A change of watch had come and gone, and then another. Chow had by then found a way to curl up and rest some, though he did not sleep. Still, he was startled when Snitch spoke.

"I found you. Bok sent me to ask why you did not relieve him," the cunning-eyed rat said. "I see why. Would you like me to chew through the rope for you?"

Chow's eyes narrowed at the rat's suggestion. To owe his escape to this rat...he shook his head. It was an indignity he would have to endure. Still, this one must die so he would not be reminded of it again. Later. For now Snitch was still useful and Chow would let him live.

"Yes," he answered.

Snitch had watched the dog's eyes, had read the humiliation and the hatred, and knew his life hung on a slender thread. But then, it always seemed to. It took all the courage he could muster, though, to come close and chew through the rope while the dog with his fangs so close watched.

As soon as the rope parted, Snitch dashed away. He was safe up a tunnel when Chow ran by. Snitch hurried to his position back at the hold's entrance. He arrived there well before Chow, having taken tunnels that let him go nearly directly while Chow had to negotiate the stairs and passageways, and keep out of the way of the human crew, lest he be tied up again. So Snitch was settled in a good position to watch when Chow arrived, breathless.

Bok ran to him immediately. "Where have you been?"

It was only half accusal, mostly curiosity.

Chow snarled, "Sharpe and I fought. The crewmen broke us up and tied us both in separate holds."

It was mostly true, though neither Snitch nor Bok knew that. For Chow to admit defeat at the hands of Sharpe...well, he just could not. "We need to kill him quickly, both of us, so that the crew do not see us. We'll do it first chance on deck, at night where we can push the body overboard."

Bok nodded, as if such a murder was a natural and ordinary thing to do. It made Snitch shudder. "No one has tried to leave since Sharpe left," Bok told Chow.

"Good. You go get dinner and water, I'll be here." And so the change of watch occurred.

Pug had refused to talk any more to them until, as he said, "I see the ship sight land, the sun rise over it, and the anchors get set. I love seeing such things."

"But the crew will tie me up again," Sharpe had said, having then to explain to Pug what had happened with Chow.

"So, the big dog thinks to kill you." Pug eyed Sharpe with respect. "He knows now he cannot do so alone, so you must be wary. He will wait his chance on deck when he and Bok can send you overboard."

"I cannot go on deck," Li had complained.

Pug had laughed. "You have once before, clinging to Sharpe, remember?" Neither of them knew how the little dog had known, but they could see he was right.

So Li had clung to Sharpe's undersides, and they had followed Pug to watch as the ship approached land. He had settled them in the bow, safely tucked into coils of rope. No crewmen had bothered them. In fact, the crew had scarcely seemed aware of them, so intent were they on their tasks. The ship was in full sail and moving rapidly through the water, hoping to sight land and bring her to safe anchorage before the new day dawned.

But it had been nearly morning, with the sea breeze quickening and the air seeming less black, nearly grey, when a sailor's cry had stirred the ship's company from bow to stern. "Land! Land, my Captain! I see it!" And then a dozen throats had taken up the cry. Men had run to the side of the ship to stare from the port side, and there as the sky gradually lightened it took shape. The Captain had taken command quickly, and the ship veered to starboard as they followed the coastline to the south, making for the anchorage and the harbor they had been told about.

Li had never imagined in her worry for Ling that she could ever sleep, and yet she started in the chill of morning, with the light from the sun making shadows everywhere, as she awakened from where she lay next to the warmth of Sharpe's soft fur. She rubbed her eyes and glanced around, making sure no crewmen were near. The sight of Pug no longer alarmed her. Though she did not trust him she knew Sharpe would protect her, so she merely watched the little dog with interest as he used his forepaws to pull himself up to look over the ship's sides at the land they were following.

"Did you see your sunrise?" She asked.

He turned and smiled. "It was beautiful, rising over low hills along the shores."

"Good, now tell me where my Ling is."

His eyes widened at her boldness, then he yipped in surprised laughter. "This is a rat to be remembered, to treasure as I do Ling," he said to Sharpe. "Is she always so bold?"

Sharpe yawned. "Yes. What of it, Pug? Where is Ling?"

Sharpe

Pug frowned now. "He is safe, as I told you. As to where, I have not decided what to do as yet, so perhaps we need to talk. The land is near, so is the anchorage, and no doubt this means your group will soon be making plans for how to get to shore. Do you really believe that you and I will be killed, Sharpe?"

Sharpe considered. He had great confidence in his own ability to survive, and so perhaps he did not think that the Emperor would succeed in having him done away with. Pug on the other hand was little and would probably not fare so well. But it did not matter. For it was not for his own sake that Sharpe had thrown in with the others. It was for Meeka. He had no doubts that even were she to be allowed to survive, she would be locked away somewhere, to be as miserable as a creature could be, thousands of miles from home, alone, and with no prospects for the future except to one day die, unloved and forgotten.

He could not allow that. If he could not get her back to her home and loved ones, which he could not, he could at least gain for her something precious, freedom. And if that meant that he, Sharpe, never got back to China, well, so be it. China had become a distant memory for him, and he knew he would be content to live among the friends he had made here on board ship.

"I do not know, Pug. It is certainly possible with the young Emperor, at least with how we knew him in port and all that we heard of him. But these others, the otters, the rats, the sloth, they will surely die."

Pug snorted. "What is that to you and I, Sharpe? We are hunters; they are the hunted. Except for the otters, of course. But we cannot worry about them."

"Can't we?"

"No."

Sharpe regarded the other with his large brown eyes. "Perhaps we should. I know that I will, Pug. I do not wish to live my life as Chow or Bok. I have decided to be a friend, to help a friend, to make a difference. Whatever you *think* will happen to us, we *know* what will no doubt happen to them. For that, I must try to do something. It is how I have decided to live my life."

The little rat catcher stared at Sharpe in amazement. His whole life he had never worried about anyone else. Pug had never had a human master to love or care about, so he did not know about caring for someone else. He had heard about it from others. Had wondered what it must be like. Sharpe had been with the old Emperor, had been loved by his handlers and felt the affection of some of his many grandchildren. Pug knew Chow had been there, too, but somehow had not experienced what Sharpe had. Knowing Chow, Pug could imagine that it had not been easy for a human to warm up to him.

"I am not you, Sharpe," Pug answered. He walked sadly away.

Li rose to follow him. Sharpe moved a paw to stop her. "Let him go. He must think."

"But he might be going back to Ling."

"Probably."

"Then we must follow, so we can rescue him." She had heard all that Sharpe had said, had understood much of it, but none of it mattered, in her mind, without rescuing Ling.

"If you want Ling to be free, you must let Pug make that choice. He will know if we follow." He sadly regarded the anxious little figure. "Li, it is the only way."

Shen-si had waited all day for the Captain. He had been taken to a spot on the forecastle, to stand quietly and wait as the Captain strode back and forth, giving orders, receiving information, working and watching as his ship made its way closer and closer to the anchorage site. The hours had gone by, soon the cry of land, the appearance of the sun, frantic action on the parts of the crew as they came nearer and nearer. Shen-si had found himself fascinated by all of it, he watched the Captain closely, he also watched the Captain's dog. To his wonder, he understood every growl from the little creature, and realized that Pek was ordering the crew around, duplicating the Captain's commands. Why, he thought, the little dog knows as much about the ship as the Captain. Then he realized something else. Pek would be invaluable to their efforts. From then on he gave the little pet his complete attention.

Pek on his part paid no mind to Shen-si, at least, not at first. He recognized the fisherman as the man who commanded the otters. But as it had nothing to do with sailing his ship, Pek had no need to recognize the man. He ignored him, concentrating on barking orders as he heard them from his master. Somehow, though, as the hours went by he became aware that the fisherman seemed to be listening to him, Pek. The little dog grew concerned. No one, not even his Captain, actually listened. He knew that. He only repeated the commands because he delighted in it, imagining that the crew obeyed his every bark. But Pek had no illusions. He knew that it was only his barks they heard, none of the crew ever responded. Men were ignorant and did not understand animals.

So why did it seem as if this one did?

But then the anchorage site was sighted and things became more frantic than ever. The Captain bellowed command after command, Pek repeating each, action became concentrated and it was long after the sun had been directly overhead, nearing the afternoon and its slow fall to the sea in fact, before the anchors were safely set and the ship lay calm and steady, sails were furrowed, and the men began to relax. It was then that the Captain turned to Shen-si.

"Fisherman," he said, "your otters have done a good job of supplying us with fresh fish from the sea."

Shen-si bowed, acknowledging the compliment, wondering what would come next. Pek wondered also.

"Now that we are close to land, my cook tells me that he would like to make the men, and me, some special dishes with shell fish. He says anemones also would be good. Can you get your otters to dive for these things?"

"Yes, Captain. They can do this."

"Good. Perhaps tomorrow." He waved a hand to indicate the conversation was finished. Shen-si bowed and began to leave.

"Why have you been listening to me?" Pek asked him suddenly.

"What?" Shen-si turned in surprise.

"I did not speak," said the Captain, "There is nothing more." He shook his head at the man, this simpleton of a fisherman, and waved again for the man to leave.

But Pek now thought what he had suspected must be true. This man knew the language of animals. From the otters, no doubt, he decided. And so, he must be working with them on their plans to wreck my ship. Pek decided that he would watch this man carefully when he came up with the otters to "fish".

Chapter 21 Bok becomes deadly

Li had found a way to follow Pug. First she had managed to get away from Sharpe, who she knew would never have allowed her to follow the little dog. She had yawned mightily and asked Sharpe if he would keep a watch while she found a safe place to sleep. The kindly dog had agreed and innocently regarded her disappearing into a hole in the deck as merely a way of doing as she had said. He sniffed and smelled her there, so he settled to nap himself.

But what he had smelled were hairs Li had torn from herself to leave a scent there. Then, as only a rat can do, she had crept away without a sound. The running that she did after that, in, around and down tunnels peeking out every hole she came to looking for Pug had her heart hammering in her tiny chest. Just when she had despaired of ever finding him, she caught sight, below her in a corridor of the ship, of his tail disappearing into one of the many compartments of the mighty vessel.

When she found the right tunnel to follow him, she managed to keep overhead, out of scent, and just barely in view of the little dog as he made his way where she was sure he had Ling. He seemed to be trying to make it impossible to be followed, she noticed, and something in his manner made her think he didn't fear her or Sharpe. She realized with a start that he was evading

Chow and Bok. So, she thought, he is not with them anymore. That is a good sign.

She nearly lost him when he entered a passage that had no tunnel overhead for her to follow, but she guessed from his direction where he would come out, then found a way to be overhead from that place and then waited, praying she would not be wrong. If he did not appear, would she ever find him again? But he appeared before panic could overtake her and she took up the chase again.

When he stopped, she nearly ran on to the next compartment anyway. At first, in the dim light where Pug had ended by sitting and beginning to lick his paws, she could see nothing else moving. Where is my Ling? She thought. Of course, she knew he would be in some kind of enclosure, but she searched and searched with eyes, ears and nose and detected nothing...no, wait, the faintest scent came to her. Yes, it was Ling!

Then Pug spoke. "How have you been, Ling?"

"Waiting for you," came the answer from an overturned crate in a corner of the room. It seemed to be a storage room of some kind, but she wasted no time worrying over that. How to get him free? The crate was heavy wood, much too heavy for a rat, or even a pair of them.

"I have been on deck with two friends of yours all night," Pug told him. "Now I am tired. I will sleep, and then we will talk."

"But, I need..."

"To let me rest, and not to make me angry," Pug interrupted him.

"As you say," Ling answered.

Then Pug did as he'd said. Li sighed and curled herself up also. She would wait, but she would also try and try to come up with a plan as she waited. She dared not leave to get help, for who knew what might happen while she was gone?

And so the day passed and evening approached. Shen-si made his way to see his otters and plan with them what to do. Chow stood guard at the hold door, waiting for Bok to return and then for a signal from Bruno to rush in and finish off the sloth and the rats. Meeka on her part calmly chewed leaves and waited for any of her friends to return, though she had made the friendship of Saraj and his rats, but they, too, were busy planning how to escape and get their families back.

On deck, the humans were blissfully unaware of the frantic animals on board the ship. For them, the preparations were to meet other humans the next day, to maintain the ship safely where it now was anchored, and the anticipation of the end of the voyage in a few months and the return to their beloved China. None of them knew their old Emperor had died, or that the new young Emperor despised them and held nothing good for them in his plans.

Bok had spent the day eating, drinking water, sleeping, and thinking about the killing he might do that evening. He felt contented, but restless for it to start. He was a born killer, relishing it and finding satisfaction in his abilities that way. Finally he knew it was time to join Chow, so he began padding along the corridor to join his comrade. But on the way he came across a piece of canvas lying in his path. In the busy bustle of finding safe harbor and anchoring the ship, none of the crew had picked it up. Each hand that came across it assumed some other sailor would tend to it.

Sniffing at it curiously, Bok suddenly became alert. His canine senses nosed all around it and put together what had happened. So, Pug had trapped Ling, then had carried him off. He had not killed the rat. The big dog's back hairs bristled. Traitor, he thought. For to him, the only thing to do with a rat was to kill it. That Pug had not, told him volumes about the little dog. In Bok's world, there were no gray areas. If Pug was not altogether with Chow, then he must be against him.

Bok picked up the trail and began to track. He would kill Ling, and Pug, too if the little dog didn't join them. When he came to the peppers Pug had spread to mask the trail, Bok did what a good hunting dog always did, he began to range wide, looking to pick the scent back up. The big dog's senses worked like they had been bred to do, they sniffed and sorted through all the many stories his nose brought him. Pug had blocked the scents on the floor, but Bok knew to sniff higher, for scents travel higher than floors. And then he picked it up where Ling had rubbed against the wall as Pug had carried him through a doorway.

In a flash, tongue hanging down and his ears standing straight up, Bok began to run along the new trail. He sniffed along the walls and found just enough to keep going. Then he smelled Pug and he slowed. Creeping now along, for he didn't want to alert the little dog, he made his way until his nose told him that Pug and Ling were in the next room. He grinned then, running his tongue over his sharp eye ripping teeth. This would be fun.

Pug heard the scratching of Bok's claws on the floor as he entered the room, but he'd been lying down and before he could react a great paw had smashed against him and swept him into the wall. Then the big dog ran past him to the crate where his nose assured him he would find Ling. Another mighty swing of a paw and the crate flew across the room. Bok looked where it had been, thinking to see the rat. Nothing was there!

For his part, Ling had not been sleeping, and so when he'd heard the big dog's paws, he had immediately leaped for the side of the crate and grabbed hold. So when the crate had been flung aside, he had been flung with it. But the power of Bok's paw had shaken him loose from it and he had crashed across it. He lay for a moment, stunned. The killer dog sniffed, quickly saw the little rat lying helpless in the overturned crate and lunged to snap his neck with one bite.

It was then that a small body landed on his head and he felt teeth ripping into his right ear. He howled and swung a paw, trying to dislodge the frantic attacker he could only feel. His first swing missed as the pain caused him to turn his own head away from where he had aimed. Before he could swing again, another small form had climbed up to his head and was biting the other ear.

Ling had come to hearing the dog howl, opened his eyes and saw his beloved Li, who had leaped from the ceiling when she saw Bok attack her mate, biting at his ear. A crazed fear for her had surged through him, giving him speed and daring to move incredibly quickly, running up a leg and onto the head to join in her attack. But Bok had been in many fights, although never with two rats biting at his ears. Still, he gathered his wits and, planting his feet, began to savagely shake his head back and forth. Once, twice and the two rats were thrown across the room, where they landed on a pile of folded canvas bags. Bok charged across at them, but they both had leapt up and, seeing a row of shelves, ran up them to stand on top, panting and eyeing the now angrily barking dog.

"Are you all right?" Ling asked Li.

She smiled, though she ached all over, because he was now safe. "I am, now that you are with me again."

"We have to get out of here," Ling told her, "his barking will bring humans, and they will find a way to kill us."

"Follow me."

She ran and jumped across a wide space to another row of shelves where he saw one open knothole. Quickly following, they both were soon safely in a tunnel. Ling gave her a quick hug, then said, "We must hurry back to the hold and warn Meeka. Bruno is going to try and kill her tonight."

Even as he spoke he began leading her away.

"How?" She asked as she followed him.

He explained and suddenly the hole above Meeka's head that she had used to escape became clear in her mind. "I know exactly where he will do that," she said. "Follow me, we can stop him."

Bruno had assembled his rats. Pietro had them ready to go down the hole, with the rope, which they would quickly put around the head of the sloth and then pull it tight. He had hoped she would be sleeping, but even if she wasn't, he knew she couldn't unwind it before her breath left her and she began to lose consciousness. If it happened quickly enough, Bruno would let the rats come back up the rope to safety. But if she pulled the rope down, or anything went wrong, he was ready to let the rope go whether they were safely back or not. Bruno knew to look out for Bruno.

He looked down the hole. Meeka sat, calmly chewing leaves. But her eyes were closed, so this would be easy. He was about to give the signal when he heard a commotion. Up from the otter hold came all of the otters and their human master. Bruno signaled for the rats to wait.

"The otters might help her. Let them leave."

They watched as the otters bid Meeka a good evening, and then all of them trundled out. Even the pup was going, Bruno saw. He remembered how strong the little otter had been and so he was glad to see him leave. Chow barked once as the group trouped out the hold opening, but the human seemed to say something to him and he quieted. When all was calm again, Bruno motioned to his rats.

"All right. Lower the rope quickly and go with it. Wrap it firmly around her throat, Pietro and I will pull from here. It should be over fast."

Meeka had watched the otters leave with hope in her eyes, but also concern. She knew there was great danger in what they were about to do. Especially she worried for Pipi. He was so young and small. She knew his parents worried even more. She waved as they left, then heaved a deep sigh. I wish Li was back, she thought. Or Sharpe. I need someone to talk to. Then she felt something wind around her throat. Sloths move slowly most of the time, and this time unfortunately was no exception. Bringing a paw up to touch it, she felt surprise. A rope. How had a rope come to be here?

But then it began to tighten, and panic came to her. Her breath began to be cut off. She brought her mighty arms up, her deep claws set to rip it apart. They couldn't find a place to grab, though, because it had become tight and her own fur had begun to fall over it. Her eyes began to see a red film come over them. She could no longer breath.

"She's dying," Bruno announced, "send word to Chow."

Pietro nodded and gave a hand sign to a rat waiting down the tunnel. He ran to tell Snitch, who remained at the entrance to the hold. But before he could get to Snitch, two rats bowled him over and ran past, heading for Bruno. They crashed into the cruel rat and the three of them fell out the hole, clawing desperately for the rope. Ling and Li managed to get enough of a hold to slide down the rope, crashing into the rats pulling it tight. They kicked together at those rats and watched them fall.

Li gasped at the face of Meeka whose eyes were now closed as she struggled to get air into her lungs. "Quick," Li cried, "she is dying."

Immediately Ling began chewing at the rope. Li did too. It was then Bruno came upon them. He swung and sent Li flying, but she fell only as far as one of Meeka's legs and scrambled back. When Bruno turned on Ling, he found the rat lunging at his throat. He threw up a paw to block him, but Ling ducked under it and pushed the rat with his head. Bruno fell. Immediately Ling attacked the rope with his teeth again.

"Back!" Bruno yelled at his rats. "Stop them from chewing the rope."

Just then into the hold burst Chow, followed by Bok who had run here from his battle with Pug, Ling and Li. The dogs took in the helpless Meeka and launched themselves at her, a killer's glee on their faces.

When Bok had flung Pug across the room he had kept his wits about him. He immediately ran out of the room and away from the crazed dog. But the blow had made him wobbly and he had been forced to pause in the corridor and take deep breaths to clear his head. He heard crashing and then frenzied barking. At first he feared the worst for Ling, but then the patter of rat feet above him told him of the rat's escape. Then he heard Ling tell Li about Bruno's plan for Meeka.

Something in Pug changed right then. He knew what he had to do, and for the first time in his life, it didn't involve doing it for himself. He ran sniffing the air to find Sharpe. He left the corridor just as Bok charged into it, running for the hold.

Pug ran hoping that Sharpe had stayed where he had last seen him. As he ran he thought about the events going on around him. Chow and Bok, he realized, were wrong. The young Emperor was certainly capable of killing all the dogs, anyone who had paid attention to him when he came to tour the ship before it was launched could have seen that. And the old Emperor had been weak and ill, so his death would not be a surprise. It must have happened as the bird had told them, for why would a bird bring such news otherwise? Pug ran harder.

Sharpe was resting as he liked to do when no action needed to be done. He conserved his energy for when it would be needed. It was his way. As Pug rushed in upon him, Sharpe felt the dog's worried energy and he rose immediately.

"What is it, Pug?" He asked.

Pug told him.

The moment he heard that Meeka's life was in danger, Sharpe was in motion. Anyone who had seen the wrinkled dog moments before would not have believed the speed with which he now moved. He might be compact and built squat and round, but once he got his muscled legs moving, he moved faster than anything Pug had ever seen. The little dog found himself panting with all his might and still hopelessly left behind.

Chow was gathering his legs under him, ready to leap at Meeka's throat and tear it apart when a growling blur of fur smashed against his side. He was flung clear across the hold. Bok, who had been ready to follow Chow's lead and tear at the sloth's throat, found himself being smashed into by a frenzied brown form that had more strength than anything he had ever encountered before.

Li paused just for a moment in biting at the rope to look at what had made the wild animal sounds below her. She saw Chow crumbled in a heap across the hold and a blur of wrinkled, brown dog fur tearing at an obviously shocked and overmatched Bok. Then her teeth had reached the other side of the rope, even as Ling's did. The rope parted away falling from the throat of Meeka. It had still been attached to the ceiling and had held the sloth up. Now she collapsed to the floor.

Chapter 22 Pek's warning

Shen-si brought the otters up one level, to a cargo room where he had hidden three sacks. He motioned to them. "You know the Captain always wants Hui, Zan and Pipi to remain in the hold, to ensure that the hunter otters will come back to the ship. At sea he might not fear so much, as where would you go? But so close to land he will enforce it. I have brought these sacks to hide them in. I will get my helpers and tell them it is some fishing equipment we need. You must be very still when they pick you up."

"But," Huang said, "Pipi is but a pup. He might make a sound or a movement without meaning to."

"I will carry Pipi," Shen-si assured her. He went to get his helpers.

Yong turned to his fellow otters. "Hui, Zan, you get in these sacks. Huang, you explain to Pipi and get him in this one."

In moments all three were safely in their sacks. Bao came up to Yong with questioning eyes. "They won't let us 'hunt' until morning. Why are we going up now?" She knew Yong and Shen-si had spent some time planning what they would do, alone and away from the others. The human had been nervous and needed, he said, to talk to only one of them at a time while planning. Yong had been chosen by Hui, and the others had given them privacy. Now they all came up to Yong to hear him answer Bao's question.

"The Master said that if he brought us up in light, then brought the three out of their sacks, someone would surely see and question. If the Captain finds out he will send them below. But in the dark of night he can safely hide them until morning. Then he hopes the crew will not count well as we go over the side."

They had already agreed about the pairings. Yong and Xun, Mei and Bao, Huang with Pipi and Hui with Zan. They were ready to go over each side and immediately begin to gnaw at the anchor ropes. There would be no hesitation, they had decided. The morning tide would carry the boat into the rocks, they hoped, before the Captain and crew would react. They hoped Meeka and the rats could get out from the hold after the crash. Shen-si had thought the ship would take hours to break apart in the crashing surf and they all could get free.

All went smoothly when Shen-si returned. He had hurried ahead of his two helpers, fastening the ropes tightly on the sacks, then directing them to take their two while he hefted the one with Pipi as Yong had pointed it out to him. It took very little time to make their way topside, and no sailors questioned them. A mate did approach as they were settled near an overturned rowing boat to wait.

"Why are the otters on deck in the night?" He asked.

Shen-si, who had commanded his helpers to leave them and return at dawn, explained to him, "At first light is the best time to get shellfish as the Captain wants. We will wait here for dawn and get a catch worthy of our noble Captain."

At these words the mate had agreed to the plan. "By all means, for the Captain then. This is good thinking, fisherman." And he left them then to tend to something on the other side of the ship.

After he left Shen-si managed to put the sacks with the other otters under the overturned boat, where they could come out and relax. Huang could hear Pipi giggling and she had to hush him more than once. She heard Zan inside doing the same.

Although they thought they would be too keyed up to sleep, all of the otters were soon dozing as the night passed.

But when the first rays of dawn hit the ship, they all came instantly awake. They found Shen-si staring at the land where the sun would appear sometime over the far mountains. "It will be a long time before we actually see the sun," he pointed out, "but there is enough light to see now." He sighed. "Emperor help me, for I hope I am not making the greatest mistake of my life."

Bao went to the kindly fisherman and nuzzled his cheek. "You are saving the lives of many grateful animals, Master. That is truly a worthy thing to do."

He brightened at that, smiling for the first time. "Yes, that is so. Are you all ready?"

They assured him they were. He lifted the boat and out crawled the three inside. Immediately everyone paired off as they had planned. Yong signaled them all. He pointed to where the anchor ropes, two on each side, were, motioned which pairs would go to each. Pausing a moment, he went to Bao and nuzzled her cheek.

"Be careful," he told her.

She smiled. "And don't you be taking those awful chances you like to either."

Then at a nod, they all ran for their respective ropes.

Pek had spent a restless night in the cabin, wondering what the fisherman was up to. They had anchored safely, everything seemed to be all right, but still a sense of danger nagged at him. As the first rays of dawn came into the cabin, he peered out the cabin window onto the deck of the ship.

It was then he saw the otters running for the anchor ropes and clambering over the sides of the ship. The anchor ropes? He wondered. Why are they going that way instead of down together in the basket as they usually did? He could see that the ropes did give them an easy way to get to the water, but then it occurred to him that the shellfish would be only on the starboard side of the ship where the rocks were. Why go over both sides?

Then he remembered all the talk from Sharpe about the new Emperor, the danger to the animals, the need to wreck the ship, and he began barking frantically to wake his Captain. It took minutes, though, to get the man awakened and aware enough to dress and follow Pek outside when he continued barking and scratching at the door.

"All right, little one, I will let you out. What can be so important?"

It was then that the ship lurched to one side and began to drift. An anchor rope, then another, then a third had broken free. He yanked the door open then and ran to look over the side of his ship. He saw otters clinging to ropes now swinging freely as they had been chewed and the weighted anchors had dropped away. Immediately he ran to the other side and saw one rope free and the other being chewed by a full sized otter and a small pup. He grabbed a truncheon he kept about his person to discipline his sailors and threw it at them, but it missed. Then the last anchor rope parted and his ship began to drift with the tide towards the deadly rocks along the shore.

The Captain began barking orders to his men. "Quickly, to the sails, unfurl some, then get the rudder. I need control, I need to steer this ship away from those rocks. Move! Move!"

With Pek barking encouragement, the stunned sailors leapt to do their Captain's bidding. The ship drifted with the tide, closing in on the rocks. But ever so slowly it began to turn away from them.

Yong saw immediately as he hung from the rope that the ship had begun to turn away from the rocks. At first when the anchor ropes had been completely cut away he had cheered because it seemed that crashing could not be denied. But he heard the Captain's frantic commands and realized the man was regaining control. He had heard Pek's barking and guessed it had been the dog who had warned him. So, he thought, Sharpe never did convince him to join us.

And now the Captain was determined to save his ship, and it looked like he might do so. In which case, he would kill the otters for what they had done, Yong realized. He prepared to tell them to jump into the sea and swim for shore. Meeka they would not be able to help, nor the dogs, he realized with a bitter taste, but at least the otters were all out of the hold and could save themselves.

Xun groaned. "If only we were bigger we could move the rudder ourselves and still send the ship into the rocks."

Yong's eyes grew wide. "Of course," he said aloud, "that's it, Xun."

"What's it?"

Yong ignored the question. "Do you see a great white fin out there anywhere?" He asked.

Xun frowned. "I hadn't thought of that. If the killer is out there, he might get us if we try to swim for shore. I hoped we could at least save ourselves."

So, Yong thought, he had thought that too. No doubt so had the others. Xun climbed higher up the rope and scanned the horizon. "I don't see him," he called with relief.

"Keep looking," Yong commanded. He called to Huang and Pipi on the other rope on this side. "Huang, look for a great white fin in the water!"

He heard her gasp. "Oh, I hope he is not out there." She began to search for it.

Agonizing minutes passed and every moment the ship turned more and more away from the rocks. Yong feared that it would not be out there when he heard a cry from the other side of the ship, from Bao who had been ready to leap into the water.

"Oh, no," she cried, "the white killer is out there!"

"Wonderful," Yong yelled, to the amazement of the other otters, and he climbed the rope, going right over Xun and up onto the deck of the ship.

The Captain caught sight of him as he ran for the other side. "Kill that traitorous otter!" He cried.

Yong sprinted across the rolling deck, dodging sailors who kicked at him or threw knives or truncheons. He came to the other side and peered out to sea. Where was the killer? Then he saw the mighty white fin off to his left. Good, he is nearer to the rudder there. Then he felt human hands grabbing at him and he dove over the side into the water. With all his strength he began swimming for the killer.

Saraj and his rats had hesitated to help save Meeka. Some wanted to, but Saraj had seen that the rats tightening the rope were Bruno's and it occurred to him that the nest might be unguarded. If they could get by Chow they might save their families. They watched the angry dog pacing outside as he heard the noise inside the hold, and guessed he would come in soon.

When Chow did charge in, with Bok right behind, Saraj saw their chance. "Quickly," he cried, "let us rush back to the nest while they are fighting."

But his rats hadn't followed him as he began to go. He turned back, staring at them. They were watching the fight as Sharpe came charging past. When Chow was flung across the hold, Saraj understood. "You feel it is our honor to help?" He asked.

They nodded.

"Then let's do so," he urged and led them back down into the hold. With a great battle cry they followed him.

The first thing they saw was Meeka on the ground, and pieces of rope around her. "Grab the rope," Saraj ordered.

The second thing Saraj had seen were Chow and Bok collapsed on the floor from Sharpe's brutal attack. In moments with Saraj shouting orders, the two dogs were bound with the rope and helpless to move as they slowly recovered. They snarled and yelped, but were unable to move. A few of the rats stood by them and kept guard, snickering.

"Not so tough tied up, are you?" One laughed.

Bok howled in rage, but he couldn't move.

Meanwhile, Saraj and some others rushed to help Meeka. She lay still on the floor while Li, Ling and Sharpe nudged her and wondered what to do. Saraj, who had seen many instances of drowning in the mighty monsoon rains of his own land, took charge.

"Roll her to her side," he commanded.

It took all of the rats and the dog to manage this, but finally they did. Then they waited, hoping and praying. Meeka lay unmoving for a long time, but finally they saw her fur begin to rise and fall around her lungs and a burbling sound came from her mouth. Her eyes fluttered, then opened slowly. She regarded the rats gathered around her, then saw Sharpe.

"Hello, Sharpe," she said softly, "what happened to me?"

They all tried to explain at once, but it was Ling who took charge. He explained about hearing Bruno's plan, then about coming to rescue her with Li. All that had happened in between he left out for another time, now he simply wanted Meeka to not worry and be better. Finally she sat up and they cheered.

Right then the ship lurched violently and everyone was thrown hard to port. It lurched again and they were tossed the other way.

"What is happening?" Li cried.

"The otters are trying to crash the ship, of course," came a voice from the hold doorway.

It was Shih.

"So, it's really happening," Ling said.

"Yes," Shih answered, "and if they succeed you had best get Meeka and yourselves on the top deck so you won't drown."

Suddenly Saraj noticed something. "Where is Bruno?"

The rat had taken the opportunity to run for his life during the fighting between the dogs. His other rats hadn't fared as well. Three had been captured by Saraj's rats, and two, including Pietro, lay dead on the floor, killed by Bok randomly as he ran into the room.

"We must get our families, now," Saraj told his rats. "We will see you when we succeed," he told those gathered around Meeka. Then he motioned to his rats and they ran off to rescue their loved ones.

"Oh, I hope he succeeds," Li breathed.

"We need to get Meeka up and moving," Sharpe, ever practical, told them.

She wobbled to her feet, then began to shuffle forward. "This will be exciting," she said, "I haven't been up for a year." Then she stopped, and her soft heart regarded Chow and Bok. "We can't leave them here to drown if the ship breaks up."

Sharpe growled. "I don't see why not."

But Shih smiled at him. "You are thinking it is best to leave them tied up for now, and I agree. But when the ship does begin to break against the rocks, I will untie them. Don't worry, I am much swifter than I look," he assured them when they began to protest, "and I swim very well."

The ship continued to lurch, fighting to right itself, Ling thought, as they helped Meeka move up deck by deck. He smiled at Li, who answered with a grin at him. What an adventure two rats had had, she thought. Then something she had once wondered about occurred to her.

"Sharpe," she said, "I once wondered about there being no female dogs on board. You never told me why."

He paused in helping his friend, then a grin came to his soft brown face. "Oh, that. Well, you see, the humans were afraid that we male dogs would fight if there were females aboard."

They followed his gaze back to the hold where Chow and Bok lay tied up. They all began to howl with laughter.

It was then that a small dog joined them. His grimace at Li and Ling tried to assure them as they backed away for a moment. "It is all right," Pug said, "I have stopped hunting rats. Right now I am more worried about the ship."

"Have you been on the top deck?" Ling asked.

Pug nodded.

"What is happening?"

"The otters have separated all of the anchor ropes and the ship was drifting to shore. It seemed as if it would crash for sure, but Pek warned his Captain in time, I'm afraid. The rudder is taking the ship back out to sea."

"Oh," Li gasped, "then you and the otters will be doomed if we get back to China!"

Pug nodded grimly. "Unless someone can work a miracle." They had paused, thinking perhaps to take Meeka back down so the Captain would not see her and do something to her. But Pug urged them to continue. "After all, miracles have been know to happen. And if I am any judge of that otter, Yong, perhaps he will find a way."

Chapter 23 The White Killer is useful

When Bao saw Yong dive from the ship and begin swimming mightily towards the great white fin, she knew immediately what he planned. None of the others could figure it out, they decided he had gone crazy. But Bao knew him, knew how he thought. He thinks he can do anything, she thought. But he can't do this alone, he is not fast enough to dodge the killer all by himself until he gets it where he needs it. She had watched him with Xun and knew how it must be. So, her heart beating like the mighty cracking of shells on rocks, she dove in too.

Yong had misgivings. He wished mightily that Xun was with him again. But there hadn't been time to explain it to his friend. Now he swam with terror in his heart, but knowing also that he had no choice. We are all dead if I can't do this, he knew. Then the white seemed to sense him, he saw the fin turn and begin to bear on him like some great, primeval vessel of doom. He turned and began to swim for the back of the boat, hoping he would feel, as he had before, the rush of water from it in time to dodge.

But when he did feel it, and when he kicked to the right suddenly and swam straight the other way, the killer stayed right on his tail, so he leapt into the air hoping to confuse it. The killer came roaring out of the water right behind him, its mighty teeth clashing frantically at the air just behind his feet, the sound alone nearly knocking him sideways. He dodged to his left this time, but it stayed right with him.

I'm not going to make it, he realized, this one is too fast. The sinking feeling in his stomach did not stop him from swimming with all of his might, but he wished so much now he had taken the time to call for Xun. Now...the rush of water behind him was so close, he knew it was only moments before he would be mashed between those knifelike teeth and ripped to pieces by the killer. He braced himself, leaping once more out of the water, the last of his strength causing his lungs to gasp for air as he did so.

Then a small, furry form flashed across the killer's nose going in another direction. The distracted shark turned away from him to pursue the new prey. Yong tread water for a moment, gasping in air and trying to regain strength in his body. Xun, he thought, you came! But then he saw the small form burst out of the water once again, barely ahead of the killer, and he saw it wasn't Xun at all, it was his dear Bao!

With renewed strength he dove to help her.

Back and forth the two of them began to play the great killer, working him ever closer to the back of the ship. Yong wanted to explain his plan to Bao, but there was never time to stop for a moment and talk. Any pause for either of them and they were dead. The white, now maddened by his failure to catch them, had begun slamming the water with its great body every time it failed to bite into either of them. Yong looked up and saw they were close.

"Follow me!" He yelled at Bao, and swam as he never had for the rudder of the ship. Reaching it, he began climbing madly, grasping at any bit of wood that stood out.

When the rudder was new he could never have done this. But over the two years of the voyage, it had been nicked and scarred enough there were dents and tears just here and there to grab and climb up. Behind him he heard Bao gasping. They were barely out of the water and only partly up it when the killer slammed into it with all its strength. The whole rudder shuddered at the impact, and then what Yong had hoped for happened. All the dents and scars, all the mighty waves crashing against it had taken their toll. The killer's great body was the final indignity it could not manage. With a great splintering, crashing sound, the rudder tore in half.

The ship, without the stability of the rudder, began to be pushed by the waves towards the rocks near the crashing surf of the shore. Soon it would be floundering on the rocks, unable to save itself.

But Yong and Bao were not watching, or celebrating. They had been thrown by the impact on the rudder far from it, into the water, back where the killer would find them any moment. They were too far down from the anchor ropes to grab them, Shen-si could never lower a basket in time, so without much hope they began swimming for the rocks. The killer, stunned for a moment by the impact of the rudder and the pieces of wood that came raining down upon it, now recovered and began circling to pick up the scent of his prey.

In moments he did. With a maddened cry of rage and triumph, he swam, mouth open and evil teeth gleaming, towards the exhausted otters. He meant to rip both apart before he ate them, and his giant mouth seemed to grin as it charged. In moments he would have them. Bao and Yong tried to be ready to leap away, but both knew their muscles were now so weakened, they trembled as they swam, there was little hope they could.

They could see the gaping mouth, the glinting teeth; they tried to gather any little strength they could for the hopeless leap. Moments from death, the killer suddenly was slammed into and pushed away from them! Two sleek, gray figures slammed into his side again, and then again. The killer moaned in agony, then in terror, trying to get free of these merciless attackers. They hit it a third time, and it was then Bao and Yong saw something they had never dreamed they would. The great white killer swimming for its life, running from its attackers, the hunted and no longer the hunter.

Their brief elation at being saved was replaced by new fear as the gray attackers turned from the white and swam towards them. What chance did they have against something that could frighten away their great enemy?

Suddenly a bottle nose burst from the water. "You all right, mate? Wicked beastie, those. Hope we were in time."

Another head, sleek, gray and smiling, came out of the waves. "Too right. Always want a chum around when one o' them appears."

Bao squealed with delight. "You're dolphins! You came just in time."

Now it was Yong's turn to give a yelp of joy. "You saved our lives. How did you know?"

Dolphins, those fun loving creatures of the sea, had always been observed by the otters as they played and fished, but few of them had come in close to shore to talk to. They had always seemed friendly, and no otter had ever been harmed by one. The stories of their kindnesses, passed down through the ages, were suddenly stories no longer.

"Saw the ship in trouble, mate, and came to watch. Never seen one so big. You trying to wreck her?"

"Crikey! Why would he do that?" His friend asked him.

"He ran the white right into the rudder."

"Just climbing it to save himself, I says. We got a bet here, bucko. What's the story?"

Bao burst out laughing, and Yong joined her. The ship was definitely now foundering on the rocks. The surf would cause it to break apart, but gently, and not before everyone could be gotten safely ashore.

"Yes, we were trying to wreck her," Yong said. He proceeded to tell their story as he and Bao rested on their backs, letting their tired muscles recover. The dolphins listened politely, adding an occasional, "you don't say," or, "fancy that."

When he finished, one of them said, "Crackin' good story, gents," then he saw Bao's expression. "sorry, gent and lady. Well, we gots to get going. My missus sent me out for a bit of shrimp hours ago. Always lose track of time, I does."

"He's easily distracted," his friend explained. "But his missus is very understanding."

"She's a good one."

And with a wave of their fins, and to the chorus of heartfelt thank-you's from Bao and Yong, the two dolphins swam away.

On board ship, Meeka and her group had just made it to the top deck when the rudder had been torn apart. The whole ship had shuddered and they had been tossed off their feet. As they rose they felt the vessel veering towards the shore, pushed by a rapid tide and rolling waves.

Pug had run to the bow to watch. The others joined him.

"Somehow Yong did it," Sharpe said.

"How do you know?" Li asked.

He shrugged.

They heard a frenzied barking then and turned to see Pek admonishing the sailors to do something, anything. But there was nothing to be done. His Captain knew it, though he still tried. Sails were unfurled to their full extent, hoping the breeze would carry the ship past the rocks. But it soon became clear they were only hurrying it that way. They were quickly taken down. It didn't matter. Gently, but insistently, the ship moved into the rocks and began to grind against them.

"We need to get off the ship," Ling told them.

"No hurry," Pug told them, glancing over the side. "We're close enough to swim to shore, I think, when it breaks apart, which won't be soon. First," he pointed, "it will settle. There's a large hole torn into the side now."

"I can't swim," Meeka informed them.

This worried them a moment, but Sharpe knew what to do. "We must go to one of the rowing boats and sit in it until the water comes to it. Then we can float to shore."

"You think the ship will fill with water that soon?" Li asked him.

He shrugged again. They made their way to one of the boats as the crew raced around them, screaming at one another, panicked by the turn of events.

Ling sat now by the small boat and felt something. "The water is filling the lower decks," he said.

They could feel it settle as water gushed into the inner holds. It was then they thought of the dogs down there, and of the rats.

Shih had felt it when the ship had begun to founder on the rocks. He went to Chow and deftly with his tiny paws worked the ropes loose. They had been wrapped thoroughly around both dogs, but not tied. The animals did not know how to tie knots. When he was free, the big dog threw a malevolent glare at Shih. "Why didn't you free me sooner?"

"So you could go and try to kill?" Shih asked.

Chow shot him an angry growl. "So I could try to save this ship."

"You don't swim well enough, my friend."

"You are not my friend."

Water had begun to seep into the hold. Soon they knew it would begin to gush in. Chow went to Bok. "Help me get him free," he ordered.

But Shih went first to him, for Chow could never handle the delicate turns of the rope with his big paws and Shih knew it, and sat. Bok growled. "Free me, small dog, or I will..."

"What you will is drown if I do not free you," Shih interrupted him quietly, "but if I do free you your anger may cause you to harm me. Do you see my problem?"

"Free him or I will harm you," Chow growled.

"No one is free who is a slave to his anger," Shih answered him. Then to Bok. "I want your word you will leave Meeka alone."

Before Bok could growl and threaten, as he surely meant to do from the look on his face, an outcropping of rock smashed through the hull in another part of the lower hold and they heard it, then the sound of water rushing into the ship. "Hurry," Bok yelped. The fear on his face replaced any anger.

Shih gave him one more thoughtful glance, then unwound the rope. The two dogs, Chow and Bok, without a thank you or a backward look at their rescuer, ran out of the hold. Shih followed, moving quickly for the water had begun pouring into the hold and would fill it fast he saw.

When Saraj and his rats reached the nest they found the rats there in a state of panic. Bruno shouted orders but no one seemed to be listening. The rocking of the ship threw them every which way. Saraj and his crew had command of the nest in short order. Bruno's rats either yelped for mercy or ran away in the face of the determined and angry rats from India. The female rats then showed Saraj something. They found a rat's body, beaten until it was nearly unrecognizable.

"Who is it?" Saraj asked.

"That betrayer, that one who told Bruno everything and caused so many good rats to die from the dogs," the females told him, anger still in their voices even as Snitch lay dead at their feet.

Bruno had seen that it was hopeless and made his usual quick escape. Saraj and crew gathered up their families and made for the upper decks.

Bruno had ducked into a tunnel and run away. He slowed when he heard no pursuit. His fear now became less than his anger. "All my plans," he moaned, "ruined by those otters, and those two traitors, Li and Ling."

In his mind he had convinced himself that Ling had turned on him. Now as he made his way, he plotted how he would get revenge. "I'll gather up my rats and we'll find a way to make a nest on shore. Then we'll bide our time. Sooner or later I'll catch Ling alone, or maybe Li, or both," he rubbed his front paws together at the thought, "then I'll teach them not to mess with Bruno."

With these sweet thoughts in his head he rushed out of the tunnel without checking first for danger, and straight into the rushing forms of Chow and Bok. Bok, fear and anger mingled in him, lunged with an angry growl at the rat and broke his neck. So ended all of Bruno's plans.

On deck the sailors saw many small boats approaching from the shore. The Maori had seen the plight of the giant ship and in their friendly way had rushed in their boats to help. The mate, who had been preparing to meet with the natives that very day, now found himself greeted by them and then working with them to coordinate the rescue of the sailors and their belongings from the ship as it slowly broke apart against the rocks. The Captain had retired to his cabin, frustrated at his inability to save his beloved vessel. While he sulked, the crew was safely put ashore.

When the Maori saw Meeka they exclaimed over her delightedly. They had never seen such a creature, and they treated her as royalty. She was carefully placed in a boat, with a watchful Sharpe never letting her out of sight, and taken to shore. The two rats, Li and Ling, managed to hide under Sharpe's furry, wrinkled hide. They stayed there, warm and safe, until all the animals were deposited on shore, then they ran to the safety of some bushes and watched as the loading and unloading of things from the ship continued.

Watching as loads were brought to the rocky beach, they saw movement erupt out of a serious of boxes brought ashore. "Look," Li pointed, "it's the rats. I think it's Saraj and his people. All their families, too. Look at the mothers and babies."

"Yes," Ling nodded. "I wonder what happened to Bruno?"

Li shuddered remembering the evil rat leader. "Nothing good I hope."

A boat brought cargo that contained larger animals. Chow and Bok, and then Shih, emerged from it, stretching their legs and surveying the land. Ling and Li ducked back into the bushes and made no sound. They saw Chow approach Sharpe where he sat with Meeka and Pug.

"Well, you got your wish," Chow growled.

Sharpe sniffed the air and sighed. "It's not China, but it is home now," he replied. "The humans here seem nice."

Bok had been watching them. "We can hunt for them," he said.

"I ought to kill you," Chow barked.

Then it was Bok who surprised them all. "Why? He was probably right. The Emperor's son, if he is now Emperor, would have killed us. Besides, the wrinkled one could have killed us in the hold. He didn't. So, we should not kill him." Then he sniffed the air again, yipped with interest and ran off to inspect the forested hills he saw.

Chow frowned, then said, "Don't expect me to be friends." He ran off to join Bok.

"When was he ever friendly, anyway?" Meeka laughed. "I don't care. It's so good to be on land again, the wind in my face. I hope the plants are ones I like."

Sharpe smiled. "They'll get over it. We are the only other dogs on shore." He smiled at Shih.

The small dog smiled back. "There is a saying. 'Even in hell old acquaintances are welcome.' I think they will learn to tolerate us at least."

"I wonder how the otters are doing?" Meeka asked.

They all pondered that, surveying the sea and trying to spot the furry forms of their friends.

Chapter 24 The Adventure begins

Yong played in the surf, riding the waves into shore over and over, Bao beside him. They frolicked and played tag, nipping at one another and wrestling in the shallow waters as the foamy waves crashed around them. Finally Bao paused, breathing hard but smiling.

"This is our new home, Yong. All of us are the only otters we will see now."

Huang glided in next to them, a smiling Pipi surfing at her side. The little pup was ecstatic to experience the shores, the waves, the surf, the beach. He had spent his whole young life locked away in the hold.

"Whee!" he cried.

Huang watched him tenderly, happiness on her face. "We are free and yes, this is our new home. But there will be other otters."

Yong was surprised. "Where will they come from?"

Zan came sliding in, following a wave as far as it would take him. Huang motioned at her mate. "Well, for one, Zan and I intend to have more pups. Perhaps you two should do the same."

Yong reared up, but the voice of his friend Xun coasting into shore made him duck down. "Give it up," Xun laughed, "we all know you and Bao will be mates. Just as Mei and I will be."

Mei snorted as she rolled in beside him. "Sure of yourself, aren't you?"

He shrugged in his calm way. "I'm the only eligible male left."

She looked indignant. "What if I don't want you?"

"Me?" He smiled. "Everyone knows I'm irresistible. How could you not want me?"

With a cry of rage she ducked his head and they began to frolick and play. The others watched them as they raced off to their left. Bao said softly, "She does really like him, he just makes her so mad with his opinion of himself."

Yong regarded her. "Does that mean you really like me, despite my opinion of myself?"

Bao shrugged. "Hard to say. Perhaps you will grow on me."

He dunked her head in the water, she did the same to him, and they rolled together until they were tired, then lay wrapped in embrace in the shallow water. Hui, the last to come ashore, watched the three couples and nodded in satisfaction. "It's not many to start a new colony, but it will do." She glanced around. "It is a good land. And the shellfish seemed fine."

Just then two funny little birds came running down from the forest. They were round and dark feathered, but didn't seem to have wings. The otters stopped to stare at them. The two birds stared back.

"What are you?" They asked.

"We're otters," Hui answered. "What are you?"

"This is our beach," one of them answered, "I'm Bert, this is Marvin. We're Kiwi."

"You're birds, aren't you?" Yong asked.

"Of course we're birds. What kind of question is that?"

"Well, you don't seem to have wings. Can you fly?"

"Of course not," Bert replied.

"Overrated ability," Marvin agreed.

"Faster on feet, I think," Bert added.

"Quite right, you tell 'em," Marvin said.

Yong had been scanning the beach, trying to figure out how large it was, where it ran. "What is this place called?" He asked the birds.

Bert ran back and forth. "This is Ruapuke. All of this. Ruapuke beach."

"That'd make you the otters of Ruapuke," Marvin intoned.

"Otters of Ruapuke," Bert rolled it around in his mouth, "has a nice ring to it."

"I'll say. Course, that makes us the Kiwi's of Ruapuke," Marvin said.

Bert shook his head. "We're just a couple of the Kiwi's. There's others. Course, there's a girl I've had my eye on, she can be *the* female Kiwi of Ruapuke anytime."

"I know just the one you mean. Bill curved just right, feathers out to here?"

"That's the one."

They kept talking about her as they ran off.

Not far away, Shen-si had been standing, listening. He had spent the morning helping their new native friends unload cargo from the ship and save all the lives aboard. The Captain remained, but he seemed in no danger and everyone decided he would come ashore when he finally had to. Pek was with him. Shen-si had not understood a word of the natives' language, though they had been all morning exchanging words and starting to learn. But he had just now delightedly understood every word of the exchange between his otters and those strange birds just now.

He sighed. The long voyage in the ship was over, but it was clear that the adventure had only just begun. Thanks to his otters, of course. The otters of Ruapuke, that is.

Postscript

The Anthropologist's Assistant marveled at the story the Maori had told her. She had recorded the whole thing as the village elder had spun it out to her. He had even demonstrated by speaking to his dog, then his cat, listening and telling her what they said in return.

Of course, who knew if he really understood their speech or merely made it up? Still, the dog had told them where to find something, according to him, and they had gone and found it there. But it all could have been planted there just to fool the foreigner, she decided.

After all, someone on the wrecked ship who knew how to talk to animals, who had taught the Maori? What a crazy story. Almost as crazy as the wreck being Chinese, the otters who fished, the giant clawed creature whose description sounded remarkably like one of the extinct giant sloths of South America.

No, she shook her head. Perhaps the Anthropologist was right. Perhaps these are only stories to make tourists wonder and buy their trinkets. She sighed. She almost erased her tapes, but then shrugged and simply packed them away. They were good stories, after all. Who knew?